STEEL
FREEDOM IN THE CAGE
BOOK II

DAKIARA

COPYRIGHT

Mind Flow Publishing & Production LLC

PO Box 48768 Cumberland, North Carolina 28331-8768

by visiting the website listed below.

Check the website for pricing.

www.mindflowpublishingproduction.com

Formatting and Cover Design by Haelah Rice Covers

Copyright © 2023 DaKiara

Mind Flow Publishing & Production LLC

ISBN PAPERBACK 978-1-951271-20-6

ISBN EBOOK 978-1-951271-19-0

DEDICATED TO MY LOVES

DaQuan, D'eja, D'ante, Kevonn and Kiara

RIP
DaQuan Jamique '95
&
Kiara Denise '00

AND TO SOME WHO HAVE GONE BEFORE ME

Mary Merriman
Burt Merriman Sr.
Naomi Thompson
Joseph H.L. Thompson
Barbara H. Whitlock

SPECIAL THANKS

To God for giving me the strength and the words to do this project.

I am blessed by the experiences to draw from. It has not always been easy.

With each project we complete, we are that much closer to touching the world. Thank you for allowing me to live my dream.

"A slow blade penetrates the shield."
No matter how long, how hard the journey, never give up... slow and steady.

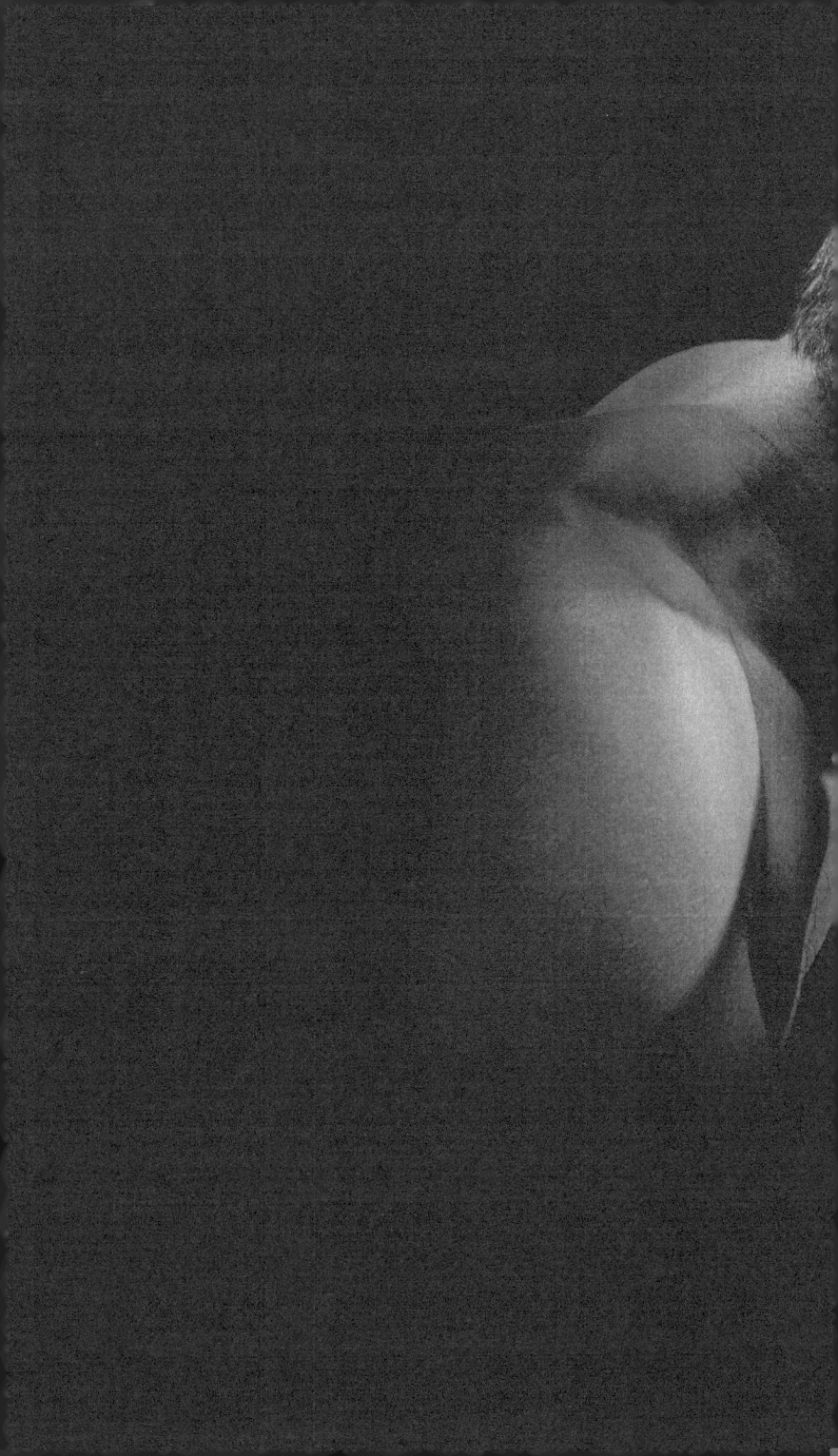

Chapter One

STEEL

Bishop Steel was a screwup, and he always had been. During his youth, he tried to sell weed and various stolen goods. He was horrible at it. The deals would usually end in him getting robbed and or beaten up. And now here he was in his cozy 8 by 6 steel cage, trying his best to keep in shape. He learned years ago that his physical shape was determined by his mental state.

This last month had been crazy. Steel made one stupid mistake that landed him sixty days in the county jail. If he messed up anymore, county would not be the end of the line. He was going straight to prison. If his grandmother could only see him now, she would be so disappointed with him. This was never the life she envisioned, nor him for that matter. Luckily, that was not possible. Steel was the last of his family. At least as far as he knew. His biological father was never around, and as far as Steel knew, he was dead. His mother never had any other children because she had a small uterus or hypoplastic uterus. He was delivered at home, and there was no time to get someone to help with a C-section. His mother Rayna bled out during the delivery, so Steel was raised by his grandmother, Isha.

He managed to get the first thirty days down without much problem. A few inmates were trying to test his limits, but they had not pushed the envelope so far. *I just want to do my time and get out of here. I'm tired of this life.*

A lot of his problems came from the fact he was a member of the 5tres. Steel got initiated into the gang when he was only twelve, and it had been nothing but craziness since then. For his initiation, he had to rob someone at gunpoint. The gang's stipulation was that it had to be someone close to you. That was their way of telling if you were serious about joining and to know they meant business if you tried to leave the gang. Of course, Steel's only family was his grandmother. He had endangered his grandma's life for three hundred bucks and a life of servitude into this gang. They didn't care about him, but only about what he could do for them.

When I get out of here, I've got to figure out how to

leave this world far behind. It has been nothing but pain and heartache.

Steel was pulled away from his thoughts when one guard yelled at him.

"Hey Steel, guess what?"

"What's up, Tony? No, I do not have any smokes. Told you that nasty habit will kill you one day. Besides, you haven't seen me have any visitors, have you?"

"You're right. No one has bothered to visit your sorry backside. But listen, they just called over and said that you were about to get released."

"What!! My time isn't up. You PoPo ain't gonna set me up. Set me free, then snatch me up when you want to for simply breathing and walking across the street. Man, I know how y'all work."

"You aren't worth the effort, Steel. Why not just stay out of trouble? Save us the aggravation of having to haul your butt in again."

The more advice Tony tried to give him; the more Steel talked back. Most people would be excited about leaving this place, and this kid was just the opposite. Steel wasn't jumping cartwheels at the thought of leaving because he knew he was heading right back to the gang. He would end up right back in a cell or dead. That at this moment was his worse fear. He would have much rather just done his time.

Steel could hear Tony buzz someone in and start yapping.

"Joshua Stone, what's happening, man? It's been five years since I've seen you?"

Tony walked from behind the desk to greet Stone, suggesting that he knew him. As the two guys hugged, Tony asked Stone if he had played any more football. Stone simply shook his head no.

"What are you doing down here? You left this place a long time ago."

"I got a call that I needed to come and bail out Bishop Steel. Do you know him?"

Tony pointed to a cell down the corridor. He started shaking his head. Tony knew Steel wasn't ready for the likes of Stone. Tony remembered how hardcore Stone was back in school. But maybe that is exactly what Steel needed.

Stone walked down the hall until Tony shook his head when he got to Steel's cell.

"Hey, man. My name is Stone, Joshua Stone. I'm here to bail you out. Are you ready to go?"

Steel looked at Stone as if he were lost. He didn't recognize this man.

"Why would you bail me out, Bro? I don't know you. I mean, I've seen you around. You are like the local celebrity and all, but we have no ties."

"Sometimes, it doesn't take a blood tie to connect

people. I see a lot of me in you. Throughout your life, you've been given the raw end of the deal. I'm here to help you. Maybe even change your life so that you can reach back later in life and change someone else's. I can show you better than I can tell you about what I'm talking about. Either way, you are a free man. No strings attached. Except you have to show back up for court. But that is really just a formality at this point."

"You run that gym downtown, right?"

"Phoenix Risen is my gym, yes. I own it, but my family and I run it together. I'd like to introduce you to everyone, and perhaps we can show you a better way to work off the negative energy. Boxing is a great way to alleviate stress. My specialty is Muay Thai, and by the way, while at the gym to help show the authorities that you are a productive citizen, I want to give you a job. Nothing too terrible, but you would clean up and lock up on some days. There are not many days where I cannot be there, but you will be called to cover when it happens. Deal?"

"I know that. As a child, I took kickboxing and Muay Thai lessons. I always go back to it when I need to relax my mind. Maybe we can spar and see what each other has. Bro, I wasn't expecting a job or any of this."

Tony walked over and unlocked the cell door.

Steel stepped out. Like the guy said, if he didn't like it, he could always leave.

"Alright, man. I'm down to learning, but there are some things we need to talk about at some point. You may not want me around after all."

The two men left the jail, and with those first tentative steps, Steel's life changed forever.

Chapter Two

BRONX

Bronx has been a member of the 5tre's for quite a while now, but he absolutely hates everything about gang life. He wants nothing more than to get out and be done with this life. There is one problem. Nobody really just up and leaves the 5tre's. They may end up in jail but still a part of the gang or die, which is really the only way out.

He thought countless times about fleeing the state and starting over, but they would have threatened his family if he didn't do everything they asked. And they meant everything. His sister Carla is in heavy with Spyder, and he is the head of the gang. Word had it that if Bronx ever disrespected the gang, someone would kill immediately Carla. Bronx often wondered how Spyder could kill her without a second thought when he professed to love her so much. What would happen to their child? Bronx and Carla's home life was screwed up enough. He vowed he would always take care of her. When they were younger, they stuck together through some crazy times. He didn't want that to be the case for his nephew. At all costs, he wanted to keep from turning to the streets as he did to feel like he belonged. That was how the gang recruited their members. They preyed on dysfunctional homes. Not his nephew. Not on his watch.

The 5tre's got word from one of their guys on the inside that Steel was released. Of course, they wanted to know why and by who.

"Bronx, what's going on? I thought I told you to keep an eye on Bishop Steel. He wasn't supposed to get out even after his time was done. I wanted him to know who controls and owns him."

Spyder wasted no time calling him up and getting in his butt about some guy he had nothing to do with. But of course, Bronx would do what he was asked to do. Like a good little soldier.

"I need you to do what you do best, well the second thing you do best, and find out where he is and who in the hell bailed him out."

"Okay, man. I got you. Who said he was released?" Bronx asked Spyder.

He figured that was the best place to start his search.

LATER THAT AFTERNOON, BRONX MADE HIS WAY TO the jail to pay Nico a visit. Nico was his cousin, a member of the 5tre's since he was sixteen. It seemed like the family tradition. One that he wished he hadn't bought into. He just couldn't take the fact that people were calling him soft. Most of the gang knew he was different, and some used it to bully him into things, while others let him be.

After signing in, the guard brought Nico into the visiting room. Nico looked shocked when he saw who was waiting for him.

"Oh shit, they sent you Bronx. Was there no one else available for this task?"

"Calm down, Nico. I just need to know what you know. You know Spyder has his quirks. Just tell me what I need to know so I can get out of here. I hate this place."

Nico and Bronx had a falling out a few months before Nico was locked up. Afterward, Nico always thought that Bronx had something to do with him getting busted. That was not the case.

Bronx cringed the moment he entered the building. His memories of this place weren't pleasant or decent at all. His first stint in was pure hell. He was locked up for boosting some cars, and they locked him in a cell for thirty days. No one from his gang or family came to visit or sent word to him at all. He was all on his own for the first time in his life.

The first week went by okay. Bronx kept mostly to himself. He didn't even look out for fellow members of the crew he knew were locked up. He was downstairs in the laundry room working on his detail, and Johnson, the guard, came down to check on him.

Johnson walked over to Bronx and made small talk for a few moments. Bronx didn't know it, but he was feeling him out.

"Why is it you have no visitors, Fish?"

Bronx hated that word. That is how they referred to new inmates. He hated it. They used it to belittle people. But he was just trying to do his bid, get out and go back to his life.

In response to Johnson's question, he just shook his head with no reply.

"What's the matter? Suddenly you can't speak or something. You know it's impolite to not acknowledge when you are being spoken to, right?"

"I don't want any trouble. You want me to talk,

fine. What would you like to talk about? I need to get back to folding this laundry. I don't want any problems."

Johnson closed the gap between them, trying to get a rise out of Bronx. He didn't react. Bronx remained calm. That didn't stop Johnson.

He stepped forward and knocked over the stack of towels that Bronx and Juju had folded.

"Oops, my bad, Fish. You should probably pick those up. I will go along with the 5-second rule. It will be our little secret about them hitting the floor."

When Bronx stooped down to pick them up, Johnson closed the gap even more, so much so that when Bronx looked up, he was face to face with John-son's *Johnson*. He let out a sigh. He couldn't believe this was happening. *Why him?*

"You like what you see, Fish? What if I made you feel it?"

Johnson loosened his belt buckle. Bronx tried to get up, but Johnson pushed him back down. As Johnson began unzipping his pants, Tony came down the steps.

"What's going on down here?"

"Nothing, man. Just playing around. You know how it is, right?"

"No.... can't say as I do. Not even close. I suggest

you get your crap together before Cap finds out about this stunt you are pulling."

Tony went and offered a hand to Bronx to help him up. Bronx shoved his hand away. His state was a fearful one, and he didn't know if Tony could be trusted. Staggering to get himself up, he ran upstairs. As he was running, he could hear Johnson's laughter echoing behind him. He later learned that Tony was a good guy. From that day on, he always kept an eye out for Bronx.

That was the reason for this memory, that laugh —he heard — coming from behind him.

"Hey, little fishy. I have missed you," he whispered to Bronx as he passed by him.

"Look, man, who bailed him out?"

"Alright, alright, but make sure you let Spyder know I held up my end. It was that boxing dude. They call him Stone, I think."

"The one who runs the gym downtown?"

"Yeah, that's him. Steel didn't seem like he knew him, though. The guard, Tony, was there. I'll see if there is anything else to find out, and if so, I'll get word to you."

Bronx decides that he needed to find out more before he reported back to Spyder. Otherwise, he knew he would get sent right back out. He decided that he would head over to the gym, ask around, see what information he could gather.

❧

When he walked inside the gym, the first thing he saw was a woman training. He watched her for a bit. She had some hands on her. He would hate to have to fight her. She'd win. Scanning the room, he saw a few others working out. There were two guys in the ring going blow for blow. Then he caught a glimpse of Steel from the corner of his eye. He was coming from what looked like an office. The place was not bad looking, could use some newer equipment but all in all, it wasn't bad.

Interrupting his thoughts, the female he spotted training walked over and asked if she could help him. By the time she was right up on him, she had her gloves off and had picked up a clipboard from the guest sign-in table. She was feminine, but strength radiated from her core. Bronx admitted he was both intimidated, yet he was captivated by her beauty.

"My name is Bronx Billings, and I'd like to sign up to join your gym. Or at least I'd like more information about it."

"My name's Jade, by the way. I have a few minutes. I can walk you through a tour if you'd like, Stone the owner, isn't here right now, but we can start on the paperwork if you like what you see."

Bronx more than liked what he saw. He hadn't had much interaction with Steel except at two parties, and it was brief. He was happy to do the tour with Jade so that he could see a bit more of him.

Jade walked Bronx through the facilities. "If you are truly interested in joining, our process is really easy," Jade said as she pointed to one of the sign-up tables. "We pride ourselves on being simple here and fairly priced. A few short forms, and you even get your own locker," she smiled coyly, then continued, "if you want special martial arts training, that will mean a visit with the head honcho, Stone."

"Sounds pretty good. What was the price again?"

"Twenty dollars a month. Unless you do training with one of the trainers, then there is an extra fee per session. We would have to see who we would pair you up with, to be more specific."

"I'm definitely interested, but mostly in just the usage of the gym."

During the tour, he kept diverting his eyes to catch glimpses of Steel. He was a handsome man. He couldn't stop staring. Jade's voice invaded his thoughts. "That guy is one of our newest members. His name is Steel. He seems to have a lot of potential when it comes to working out and possibly fighting."

Trying to lighten the moment, Bronx says, "Yeah, I saw that you have some hands on you. I'd hate to be on the end of those. I'm not a boxer, but I can tell your jabs have power behind them."

"Thank you," Jade smiled shyly.

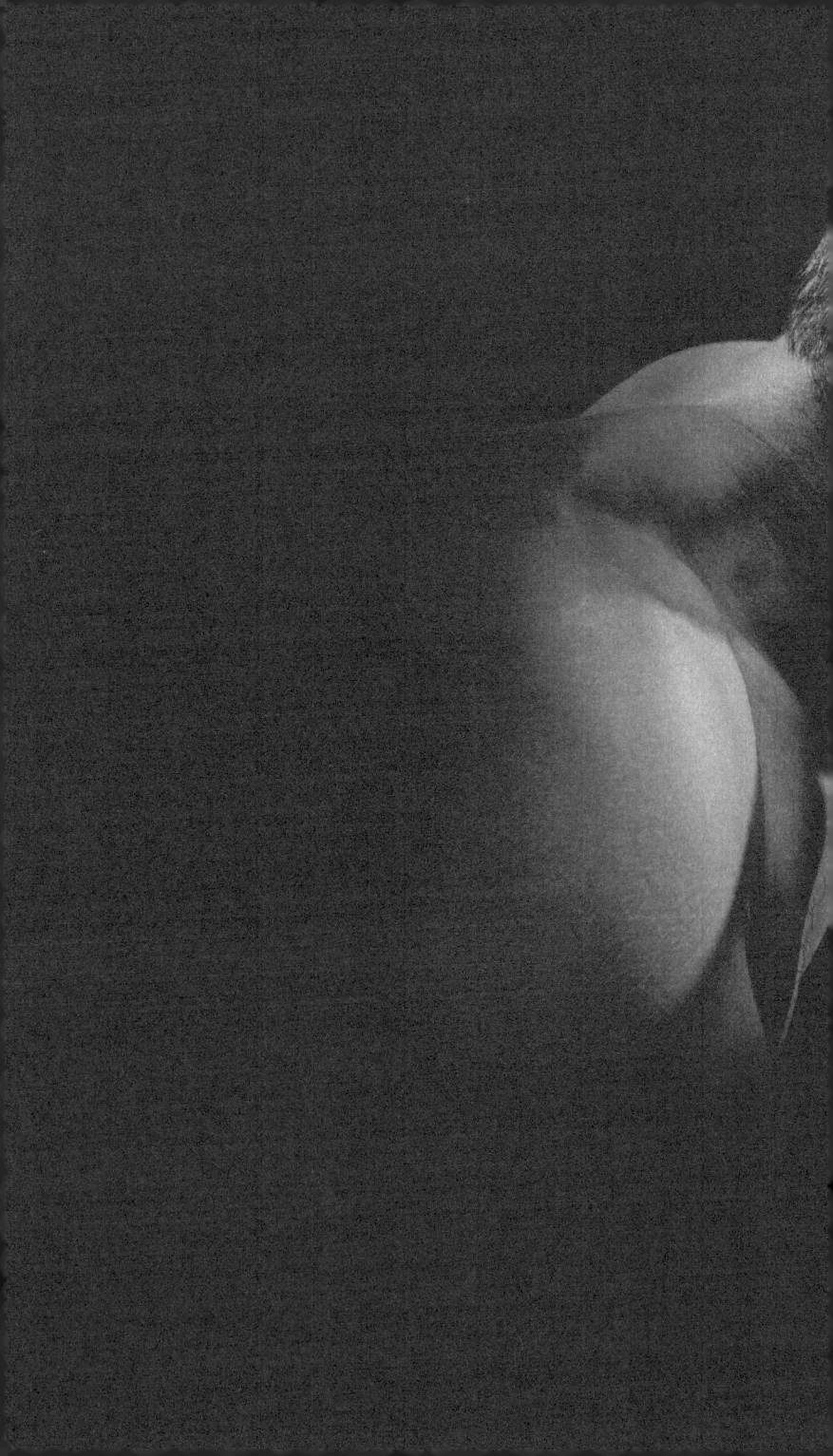

Chapter Three

STEEL

A few days go by, and Steel has begun his training. He had gotten to know Stone a bit more and discovered more about his background. It was an honor to be trained by him. Steel still didn't know why Stone put his neck on the line while bailing him out. So far, he had heard nothing from his crew, but he knew it wouldn't be long. Spyder enjoyed knowing where all his cronies were at, even when you weren't in his direct circle.

Every time he hung out at the gym, he spotted Brick. Just a few short years ago, Brick was *the man*. The prime contender for the championship belt, but it didn't go that well for him. He seemed to be bouncing back, though. *Maybe one day I will be as good as he was, if not better.*

"Why are you always watching Brick like a hawk? He is one of my greatest fighters."

"I know. That's why I'm watching. I've been studying his moves. I'd like to be as good of a fighter as he was back in the day."

"Back in the day? Don't sleep on my guy. He still has it. He has just been slow to use his gifts. But, between you and me, we are staging a comeback. Flint over there; he, too, is working on getting ready for his next fight. Jade there just had her first one and killed it. We've been scouting some other ladies to add to our ranks as well. Eventually, Phoenix Risen will rise again."

Steel saw the love on Stone's face for his gym. It made him feel good to be a part of its resurrection.

"I know you are eager to fight, but we need to work our way up to that. Fighting properly without a lot of risk for injury isn't easy. Nor is it something you can just jump into but trust me when you are ready. I will make the call and get you some exhibition fights set up. You have to just trust me; it is a process. I will train you to control your anger and fight with your emotions and your mind. Our goal is never to end someone's career because we have all seen how it has broken Brick down. It's taken him two years to build himself back up, and he was fighting for years. For now, we focus on laying the groundwork for your training."

Steel knew that what Stone said was true. He would follow his lead. So far, he hadn't steered him wrong.

"Hey Stone, I never really told you thank you for bailing me out. I truly appreciate everything you've done, sticking your neck out for me and all. You looked out, and you didn't have to. An angel must have sent you, my way. I do have a favor to ask of you, though."

"What's up man, we are supposed to be training. You are doing a lot of yapping. How you going to be one of the greats?"

Steel laughed out loud.

"See, man, I'm trying to be serious. My court date is coming up next week. I wanted to know if you would come along with me. You know, for moral support. I don't want to go back inside."

At that moment, Stone could see a little of himself in Steel.

"Of course, I'll go with you. Besides, I have to make sure you don't run on me. You look like you would be fast on your feet. Don't worry. We will get through this. We have all screwed up. That is just a part of life. What matters is how we bounce back from screwing up. You're going to be just fine, kid." Stone said, laughing.

Steel trained daily for the better part of the day. Stone would often say he was like Flint, which was a good thing. Stone told him how far Flint had come in his training since he started and wanted nothing more than a shot at a fight, so he trained his butt off, and no matter how well he trained, he still almost lost.

"Not only your body must be ready, but your mind too. It will play tricks on you."

Over the next few days, Steel takes notice of Bronx always hanging around the gym. He looked familiar to him, but he couldn't place where he knew him from. The guy doesn't seem to work out much, but he's just always there. Around the fifth day, he walked over to him and struck up a conversation.

"Hey, Boss man. How's it going?"

"Hey, what's up? It is going okay so far. Trying to get the hang of things. That is, if I do not kill myself first," Bronx said while laughing.

"Any time you need help, and I'm here, just let me know. I'll do what I can."

"Appreciate that man. Everybody here has been pretty friendly so far, and that means a lot."

Bronx extended his hand out towards Steel, who accepted it and shook it firmly.

Steel turned and walked away with that, but he

was intrigued about the tingle he felt as they shook hands. Steel tried to brush it off and get his mind back to his training, determined to remember where he knew him from.

Chapter Four

BRONX

Bronx spent more and more time around the gym, making fewer trips to the normal hangouts of the gang. About a week after getting his assignment, he stopped home to his mom's house. Since joining the gym, he stayed at a hotel just around the corner. Before he could even open the door, he was tapped on the shoulder. He turned around quickly to see one of Spyder's guys.

"What gives man? Why are you at my house? That breaks the rules. Even Spyder has to acknowledge his own rules."

"That's why I'm here, actually. Spyder said, you have been MIA, so I came to find you. He says he wants something, and you are the one who has it. Just come with me, and it will be over soon. He just wants to know what you know. That's all."

Bronx was no dummy. He knew it was never going to

be that simple when dealing with Spyder. But he would do almost anything to keep the gang stuff away from his mother's front door. Charlie just so happened to be the one who assaulted his mother during the robbery for his initiation. Bronx knew how Spyder's mind worked. He was almost certain that was why this guy came looking for him. He could only imagine the look on his mother's face if she recognized him when opening the door.

"Give me a second, man. I need to go check on something." Bronx hoped Charlie would just leave. It didn't work.

"Take your time, kid, just not too much," As Bronx turned to walk into the house, Charlie added, "She's doing well, by the way."

Bronx heard his disgusting laugh even after he closed the door behind him. Usually, his mom would be in the kitchen cooking at this time of day, but she was not. He became a little anxious as he walked through the house, looking for her. He didn't want to call out in case he frightened her. His heartbeat returned to normal slowly after seeing her in her bed resting. He hated to admit that she was starting to look as if life was beginning to catch up with her.

"Momma?" he tapped her on the shoulder. He didn't really want to wake her, but she had a thing about people being in the house. Strangely enough, she would know someone was there, but it would bother her all day until she figured out who. Bronx didn't want her to worry someone had broken in.

"Momma?"

Slowly, she opened her eyes. As they adjusted, she recognized that it was Bronx. She reached out to him for a hug.

"My son, I'm so glad to see you. Where have you been? You know I worry about you. Stand back, let me look at you."

Bronx did as he was told. He knew she was going to say he needed to eat more. That was her thing. She always thought he was too thin.

"What have you been eating? Nothing, that is what it seems like. Your are skin and bones. Let me get up, and I will fix something for you to eat right now."

"No, Momma, I'm okay. I've been eating, I promise. You get some rest, and I will come back later, okay?"

She nodded, but he knew she was not happy. Bronx bent down and gave her a kiss on the forehead, and she smiled. Bronx turned and walked away, calling back over his shoulder, "I love you, Momma. See you later."

When he opened the door, he half expected

Charlie to have gotten tired of waiting and decided to leave, but no such luck.

"There you go. I thought I was going to have to come in and get you myself. I have already called and told Spyder that we were on our way, so let's get to it. He says he has other things to do."

Bronx had an uneasy feeling about this, but there was nothing he could do. He followed Charlie to his burgundy Dodge Ram pickup truck and got in the passenger side. They rode in silence for about forty-five minutes.

The drive would have only been about twenty-five, but some heavy traffic held them up.

When they finally came to an abrupt stop, they were outside the gang's hangout, an abandoned warehouse that Spyder had converted to their playhouse. He had the guy turn the lights and water on and even the cable, but never paid one cent for any of it. No one from those utility companies ever came to inquire, either.

As they ushered Bronx into the lair, he spotted Spyder as he approached him, along with about five other guys flanking him.

"So Bronx, you don't write, you don't call. What am I to think? You don't love your family anymore?"

"Nah, man, it's nothing like that. I've just been

trying to get the information you wanted. It has kept me pretty busy."

"Okay then, that is great. Let's have it. Whatcha got for me? You must have gathered a lot because we haven't heard from you."

"That's just the thing. There isn't much to tell. I haven't gotten close enough to find out specifics other than he didn't know this guy, Stone. He said the guy did someone else a solid in getting him out. I just don't see a lot there."

"That would be why you're not the brains of this operation. I think you know more, and you are just not telling us. Why you would do something as reckless as that, for the life of me, I don't know."

Spyder gave a subtle head nod, and the group of guys surrounded Bronx. He backed up without realizing there was a wall behind him.

"Come on, Spyder, I told you what I know. Call off the goon squad."

Charlie punched him in the stomach first, and then the others took their turns. After a few blows, they forced him to the concrete floor, clutching his stomach, but they didn't stop. They stomped on him. Bronx caught a view of Spyder from his peripheral vision, and judging by the look on his face, he was enjoying this. This was one reason Bronx wanted out.

Just for kicks, they were doing whatever this man said to do.

"Enough," Spyder finally yelled out, and they stopped immediately. "You are tough, kid. I'll give you that, but how tough is your sister? I'm only going to say this once, so listen carefully. If you don't bring me back something I can use, your sister will be the first to deal with the consequences of your actions, or lack thereof."

"You are an evil man. So, help me if you hurt my sister, I will kill you, and it doesn't matter how many guys you send, they won't be able to stop me."

Bronx knew it was a big no-no to threaten Spyder, but he felt he had no other choice. Besides, he meant what he said. He didn't know how he would pull it off at that point, but he wouldn't stop until either he was dead, or Spyder was.

"Get this joker out of my sight," Spyder hollered as he turned on his heel. Turning back to look over his shoulder, his gaze found Bronx. "Get out of here and don't come back until you have something useful for me." With a look of disgust on his face, he paused before continuing, "But don't let it take too long; otherwise, dear sweet mom might receive packages in the mail. That would be just wrong."

One of the other guys helped Charlie get Bronx's battered body into the truck, and he dropped him a few blocks from the gym. As Bronx made his way out of the truck, Charlie spoke up.

"Hey kid, take care of yourself. You are lucky that you are still intact. I will give it to you. You have a set of balls on you. You have made yourself a dangerous enemy by threatening Spyder. To be honest, I am surprised you are still breathing. God is on your side today. I've seen him kill for so much less," he spoke in an almost endearing tone.

Bronx knew Charlie was right. It didn't mean he had to like it, though. He knew he would do what he needed to save his family in the end.

He made his way to the gym and headed straight for the locker room, hoping no one would see him or come in, at least until he had time to clean himself up. He knew he had to hurry. It was getting late, and the last few stragglers would head to the showers soon.

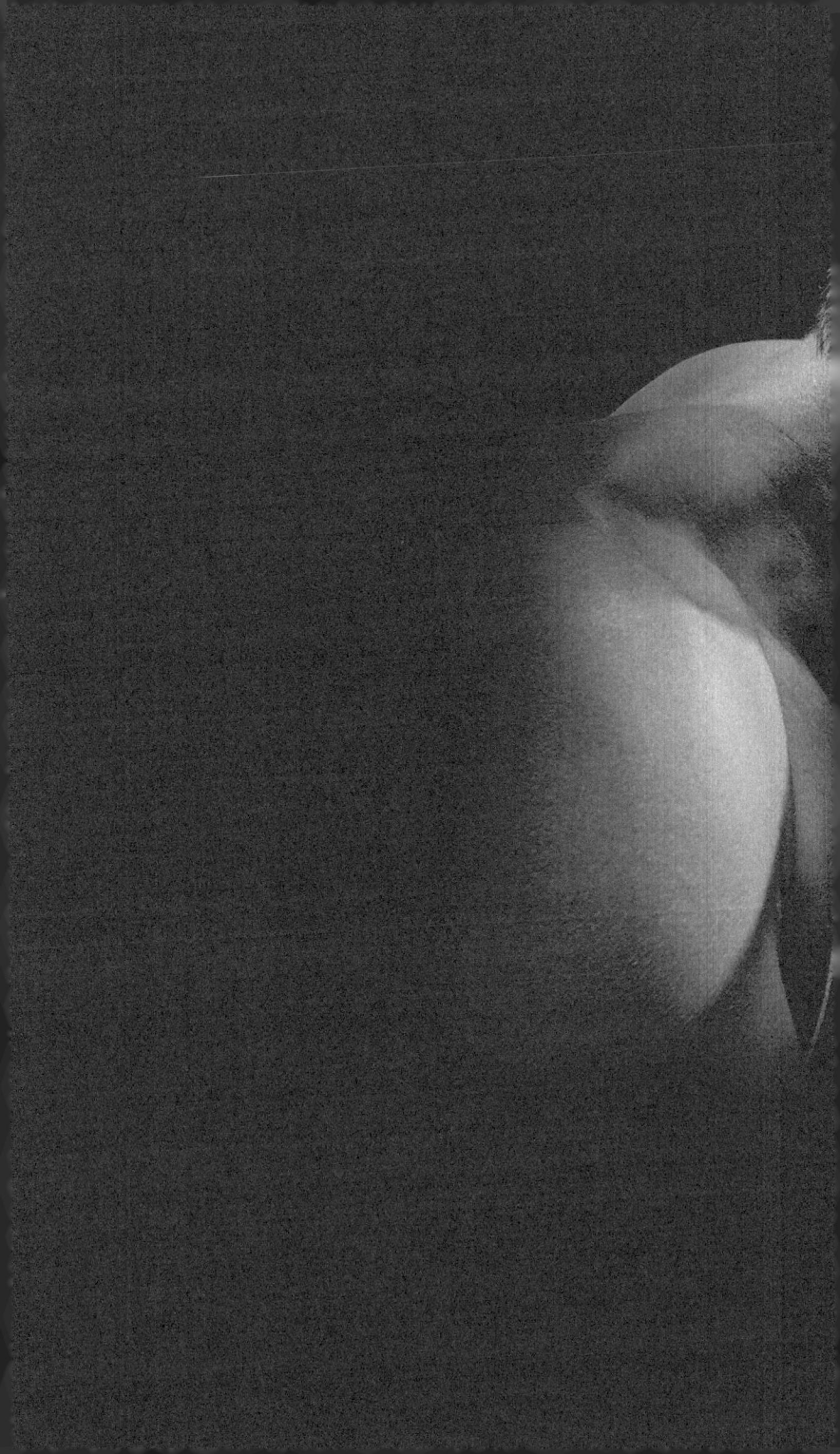

Chapter Five

STEEL

The last few days, Steel had been giving his all during his workouts, and Stone was right. He was feeling a little better, less stressed. He was still concerned that they would put him back inside when he went to court. That was not where he wanted to be, at least not anymore.

He tried to push the negative thoughts from his mind and only focus on what good was to come. Steel knew he needed to talk to Stone about the gang. The last thing he wanted was to bring trouble to this man's gym. He decided he would talk to him tomorrow; he could not see wasting any more time with it. If Stone wanted him gone, then it was best to figure that out early on before they both invested too much time in each other.

Steel was so deep in thought that he did not even see Flint until he was right up on him.

"Hey man, are you good? You looked like you were in another world there for a minute," Flint asked as he jabbed him in the back playfully.

"Yeah, man, I'm good. Just need to clear some stuff off my mind. Have you seen Stone in the last few minutes?"

"He and Brick left about an hour ago, man. Do you need something? Need me to call him?"

"Oh no, it's cool. I will just talk to him tomorrow. No need to disturb him. But thanks, man."

Without another word, Flint slung his gym bag over his shoulder, headed for the front door, and left for the night. Steel decided it was time for him to get while the getting was good. As he headed towards the shower, he could hear someone yelling out in pain. He pushed the door to the locker room open, and his eyes fell on the new guy, Bronx, trying to wrap his stomach area.

He rushed over to help the guy; it was clear to see that he was in terrible shape.

"Hey man, let me help you with that. Did someone here do that to you? The rules are no excessive force."

At first, Bronx did not want to offer up any information. He did not want Steel to freak out or tell Stone or the others what he was doing. It took everything in him to allow this man to touch him. Bronx should have been concentrating on the pain, but he could not deny Steel's touch even through the pain. Although Bronx had never been with a guy, he knew something heavily attracted him to some, and Steel was one of them. Unfortunately for Bronx, the attraction was getting stronger by the day.

"Are you going to tell me what happened, or are you going to let me just keep guessing? Trust me, I can come up with some stuff."

"I kind of got into it with some guys. There were six of them and only one of me. You know what that adds up to, exactly what you see here. Exhibit A, as in an old-fashioned ass-whooping. I appreciate your help in getting me cleaned up. You should let me repay you," Bronx said as he winced in pain. "Have you had dinner yet? Maybe we can go grab a bite before it becomes too late to eat."

"Nah, I haven't eaten yet. That sounds like a plan but let me finish getting you wrapped up first. Otherwise, you probably will not make it anywhere. I remember someone cracked a few of my ribs as well, just a few years ago. But I'm all done with that life. Whatever you have going on, man, it does not have to be that way. Just know that."

Steel continued to wrap him up after he went and

retrieved more ACE bandages and some antiseptic from the medicine chest. He had grabbed a few Band-Aids for the cuts that were on his face. Steel thought to himself, *how could this man be worried about food when he looked like someone's personal punching bag, and he had to feel like it too.* He had his own reasons for agreeing to dinner. Maybe he would finally figure out where he knew him from.

"Hey man, this crew that did this to you. Have you told Stone or anybody about it? He is pretty good at fixing issues, trust me. The guy has been a lifesaver in my short time here. I would not trade him or this gym for anything."

"Nah, this is just something I have to deal with. Besides, I've only briefly spoken with the owner. I definitely need some training so I can defend myself," Bronx sighed. "Everyone has been pretty chill here, and I'd like to keep it that way."

"I can respect that. If you ever need to talk, I'm here." Steel stated. To lighten the heavy turn of the conversation, he continued, "So this dinner, is it all you can eat? Or am I limited to a sandwich or something light?" Steel laughed as he joked.

Bronx wanted to laugh, but when he did, the pain made him wince instead.

"Maybe we should get you to the hospital and take a rain check on the food. What do you think?"

"I'm good man. I owe you, and I plan on paying off my debts."

Steel shrugged his shoulders and told Bronx if he was sure.

He finished getting him bandaged and left him to gather himself while he went and gathered his own gear for the evening. He was tired, but he still wanted in on this meal. There was something about that guy, and he could not quite get a read on the situation. Never once did it cross his mind, Bronx's real reason for being there.

Bronx hobbled out of the locker room, yelling out, "I'm ready to go, man. No rush, but I will wait for you outside."

"Alright, I'll be out in a few. I just have to lock up," Steel called back.

"You need me to take anything out for you?"

"Nah, I'm straight," Steel spoke again.

Steel was the last to leave the gym, so he had to make sure the place was secure. The last thing he needed was to deal with Stone over someone breaking in and vandalizing the place. He was many things, but foolish was not one of them. As he was doing his last walkthrough and turning off lights and equipment, he saw a crumpled-up piece of paper on the floor. Grabbing it up, he opened it to find a telephone number. The number looked familiar, as it belonged to Spyder. It was to one of his burner phones. Not sure if it fell from his pocket or from someone else's, he knew it was a sign that he had to talk to Stone in the morning. Steel remembered he was going to enjoy a meal with Bronx and a smile crept to his face. He will deal with that tomorrow.

Chapter Six

BRONX

Bronx could not believe Steel had said *yes*. He just threw the invite out, not expecting him to accept, but when he did, Bronx almost forgot to breathe. His nerves were getting the best of him as he sat outside on the hood of his Carolina blue Toyota Camry, waiting for Steel to come out of the gym. *Why couldn't this just be a normal dinner? One where I was just getting to know this guy because he interests me, not because of no bull crap orders from Spyder.* Bronx was determined to complete whatever assignment he needed to so that he could keep his sister free of his clutches. He feared she would not come easily. When Bronx looked up and saw Steel coming from the building, his mind went blank for a moment. *If only this was a perfect world. I have never had an attraction such as this before, and he has no idea.* Bronx had always been bullied for being different. He had gotten used to it.

"You ready to go finally?" Bronx called out to Steel as he walked towards his car. Within seconds, Bronx had slid into the driver's seat with a kid-like grin on his face.

Steel only smiled and nodded. He opened the door handle to get inside the car, and his attention was taken away briefly as he heard another car's engine start-up, but he could not see where it was parked. A moment later, a dark SUV with no lights rolled past as he sat in the seat and was putting on his seat belt. An uneasy feeling grabbed hold of him, but he quickly dismissed it. This was one of the first times he thought maybe Spyder was lurking just out of sight. Could it have been a coincidence finding his number and then this? Steel was never one to believe in coincidences. He always felt that things were just not random in the way they happened. When he was incarcerated, he became suspicious of everything and everyone.

Since his release, he had felt comfortable for the first time in his life. Things seemed to have been going well with him being at the gym. Stone treated him as family, as did most of the other regulars. While incarcerated, he always felt he was looking over his shoulder because he did what many of the 5tres couldn't. He was staying under their radar.

Bronx tapped him on the thigh. Steel nearly jumped from his seat, with the seat belt and all. He was so startled that he was borderline embarrassed.

"I'm so sorry, dude. Are you okay? You zoned out on me, but I had no idea you were that far gone. If we need to do this another time, it is fine by me," Bronx was starting to get concerned about Steel. In his observations, he had never seen him shaken like this.

As he sheepishly rubbed his head, he kept apologizing to Bronx. "I'm the one who should be sorry. Not sure what just happened there, but I will get it sorted out. I appreciate you bearing with me. I think I'm okay to go ahead to grab some dinner. I am a little tired but have not eaten. So it is either now or be back up and out later, and it is getting too late for that. So, let's go."

Bronx nodded understanding started the car up, and eased into the street. He had been so enthralled in Steel's movements he hadn't noticed the SUV, so he really had no clue as to what just happened.

Steel pulled his phone out of his pocket, pulled up Stone's number in his contact list, and sent him a quick text asking to meet him tomorrow at the gym. Stone responded immediately with a simple thumbs-up. That added a little relief to Steel's thoughts.

"You calling some company to join us?" Bronx joked.

"Nah, not this time. I was just checking in with Stone. I can call a few people to come to hang out if you like. Not sure what the response would be at this time of night, but...."

"I'm cool, dude. Maybe next time."

A part of him was relieved that Steel had not called in backup. It was a short ride to the restaurant, and Steel was jumping from the car before Bronx completely stopped. Either this guy was super hungry, or he was bugging out. *What if he knows that Spyder has put me up to something?* This was confusing enough for him to try to keep his feelings in order. He already felt bad about having to do it.

The two were seated right away. With no hesitation, they both ordered the special. The waiter brought them water to sip on while they waited.

"Steel, how did you get into this MMA and boxing world?"

Steel began to talk freely about the gang and how he had been mixed up in that world for a while, but that he wanted no more part of it. That wasn't the life he was cut out for. It could not be. Otherwise, he knew he would always get caught or in trouble. Which led him to this point. After being in jail this last time, he was determined to make a fresh start and do right.

"I knew I had made the wrong choice when my initiation involved robbing my grandmother. On the night of the robbery, she was coming home from playing bingo, and she was assaulted with a pistol because she would not give up her purse. I didn't know it at the time, but she had just withdrawn money to take me on a trip to Disneyland earlier that day. She tested her luck at bingo to see if she could win more, and she did. Granny had over three thousand dollars in her purse that night."

Bronx was a little disheartened that Steel was giving him information on top of more information. *How could he be so trusting? Does he not know that Spyder is relentless?* A part of him wanted to stop asking questions. Steel was a good guy who just got caught up in life in the streets from what he had seen. He deserved a way out. His thoughts drift to Carla. She deserved better, no doubt. The code has always been family over everyone and everything. He had promised himself that he would always protect her, and that was a promise he was determined to keep.

"Dude, you still with me?"

"Yeah, man. Sorry about that. I was just thinking about my sister. I don't spend enough time with her these days. I have to change that. Life is too short. What about you, Bro? You got a family?"

Steel told him about his almost nonexistent family life. "It was just me growing up. My mom died when I was born. I don't know much about my father. As far as I know, he is dead to me. It has always been just my grandmother and me. That was up until about six years ago when she passed away from a heart attack. It wasn't until after the funeral, trying to go through all of her affairs, that I found out I was adopted." As he was talking, he looked down at his phone. There was a message back from Stone saying he wanted to see him in the morning as well.

"Adopted? Are you okay with that?" Bronx inquired.

"I have no choice but to be. I am okay with my life. It wasn't always bad. Some of it, if not all of it, was my choices."

"When will you get a fight? Do you have anything on the books yet, or do you think you are ready for one?" Bronx felt he needed to change the subject.

Steel shrugged his shoulders.

"I don't know if I am truly ready for one. I guess truthfully, I won't know that until I am in the ring, either taking notes or giving them. I have been training pretty hard, but I know it takes more than training. I trust Stone in that arena. He has been doing this a long time, and I know he will let me know when he feels I am ready."

The pair continue chatting while finishing up their meal. The whole conversation was pleasant, and Bronx kept feeling moments of regret at nosing around into his life, although he did want to learn everything he possibly could know about this man.

"You are going back to the gym, or do I need to drop you somewhere?" Bronx asked, thinking he would get an invitation to Steel's place or at least know where he lived, but no such luck. *Couldn't blame a guy for trying.*

He would have to settle for the information he gathered and decide when and how to present it to Spyder.

"The gym is fine, man. I appreciate it. I have my car today. I enjoyed the food, and the company wasn't so bad either," Steel said with a smile on his face.

The ride to the gym was made in silence, each of them held captive in their own thoughts. Steel felt it was easy to talk to Bronx, and he didn't understand completely why. He also wondered if Stone would be okay with his past slowly creeping its way into his future.

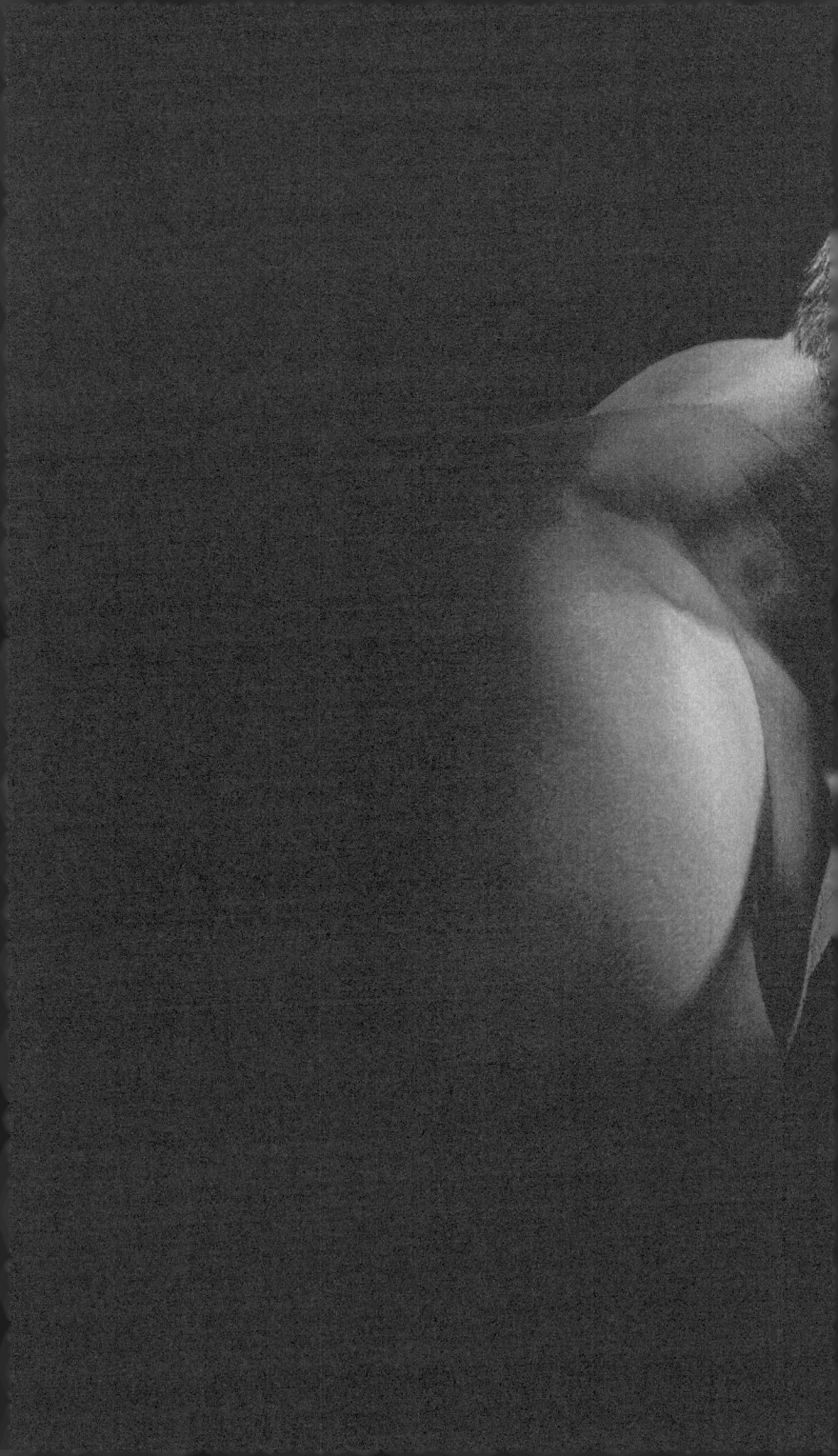

Chapter Seven

STEEL

Steel was a ball of nerves knowing that today was going to be the day that he had to lay all his cards out on the table and be prepared to accept the consequences from Stone. He arrived early because he couldn't sleep. At least he thought he was arriving early enough to open the gym and get things prepared for the day. No such luck. Stone was already at the gym working with a client, which he rarely did this early in the morning. *Was this a bad sign?*

"Good morning, Bro," Stone called out as he was entering the gym, trying to quietly close the door behind himself. He was trying his best not to capture any attention just yet.

"Hey man, I didn't know you were going to be in here this early. Thought I could come in and get me a good solid pre-workout before you guys started arriving. Good thing I didn't arrive naked, huh?"

Stone and his client both laughed.

"Go ahead and get to work. We will catch up later today. I have a few errands I need to run after this session, but I will be back."

Steel was thankful that Stone was preoccupied. That gave him more time to get his thoughts together. Steel did some running on the treadmill after stretching to loosen up his legs and get his cardio. Since becoming a part of the gym and working under Stone's training regime, his workout sessions became more intense. He was enjoying it and what it was doing for his physique.

Steel had never been overweight, but this regiment was adding more definition to his already toned body. Honestly, he loved it and the looks he often received.

After a few hours had passed, Steel was tempted to go home. He had pushed himself to new limits today. Steel sparred with Flint. Of course, Flint won, but he showed him a few moves that he would now work to master.

Steel was sitting down on the mat and doing some stretches, trying to cool down, when he saw Stone coming his way. Immediately, his nerves began to roil in his stomach, but he was determined to go through with it.

Stone walked over and sat down across from him. "What's going on, brother? I sense something, but I do not know what it is. I know you've got something weighing heavily on your mind," looking Steel straight on in the face, he asked, "You ready to get it over with?"

Steel nodded and asked if they could go to the office away from prying ears. Stone got up and extended a hand to Steel to pull up off the mat.

Steel began talking before they made it all the way inside the office. It felt as if the faucet had been turned on, and all his secrets came flowing out.

"Stone, I can't tell you enough how much I appreciate everything you have done for me. From bailing me out to giving me something else to believe in and work towards. I want to make sure that all my cards are on the table. I do not know what all you know about me, but there is this gang, and when I was younger, I got caught up in that lifestyle. I have tried the life of crime, and obviously, I am no good at it. I keep getting caught. For the life of me, I have been trying to get away from them. Away from that negativity, but I feel like they are not through with me yet."

Stone had been quiet as Steel was talking. This was a story he had heard many times from different kids, but he believed in Steel and that he was on the up and up.

"What do you need from me, bro?"

"I guess I just wanted you to know. They may come after me. I just have a feeling they are not going to let bygones be bygones. If you think I should leave so as not to bring drama to your space, to your home, then I will."

Steel told him of the different little things he had noticed over the last few days, from the SUV to the phone number, to just the weird feeling he was having, like he was being watched.

"All I want to do is become good enough at this fight thing to make some money and have fun."

Stone was with him until he spoke about the money. "Kid, in this arena, yeah, it is good to make money, but you have to have a love for this life. It damn sure isn't easy. It's not easy coming in here day after day. Dedicating yourself to training only to never get a chance at a fight or the opposite, be at the top of your game, and get hurt. I would advise that if you are going to do this, you find a reason to live this life other than to get rich or famous. In this sport, you can lose your life if you aren't careful."

"So, do I need to leave the gym, or am I good to stay?"

"We don't go looking for trouble, but we do know a thing or two about ending it, though. If you tell me you are done with the gang world, then you are safe here. Most people know not to bring drama to my front, back, or side door. I knew some of what you told me already. It was my choice to bring you in. I don't regret it."

At that moment, it felt as if a great weight had been lifted from Steel's shoulders. He sighed a long sigh of relief. Steel stood up, getting ready to walk out of the office, when Stone spoke up again.

"Now, if you are done with all the pity party BS, I got some good news for you. But only if you are ready to hear it."

"What is the good news, bro? I could use some of that in my life right now. I thank you for being so understanding of what I have going on. You have made me feel like part of a family. Almost as if you are my big brother. That is something that I have not had in my life. But anyway, back to this news. What are you holding on to? I would like to know."

"Well, brother, how prepped do you think you are for a fight? Not a sparring match with me, but a real match?"

Steel couldn't believe his ears. A grin spread across his face as if it were Christmas morning, and he got the gift he had asked for all year long. He was so excited that he started stuttering.

"OMG, dude, I would love to say that I'm ready, but I know I'm not just yet. Tell me what I need to do, and I will do it. I want this shot so much."

Stone wanted to believe that Steel would do what was needed to get himself ready to hop in the ring. He agreed he didn't think he was there yet, although he had been working really hard. Even the other guys saw how hard he had been throwing himself into his training and conditioning.

"I believe you, and it is going to take more work." He motioned for Flint to come in as he was by the door at that time. "Flint is going to work with you, as well as myself. I asked Flint to come in to tell you about his first fight and what to expect. His first experience was interesting and a great learning experience, but I will leave him to chat it up with you about it. I'm going home. If you need me, you know how to find me." Stone stood and clapped Flint on his shoulder before leaving the office, letting the door close with a bang behind him.

Steel still was in disbelief that this opportunity was coming sooner rather than later. Flint recognized the look on his face. It was the same look that he had not that long ago.

"Hey man, look, I've sparred with you, so I pretty

much know what you are capable of at this point. I would encourage you to definitely put some more work in before the fight. I went in thinking that I was ready, and I will admit that I was a little cocky, and I nearly kissed the mat."

"What do you mean? I heard that you won your first match. Everyone talks about it."

Flint snickered a little, and a snort escaped his mouth. "I got lucky. I ran in with a clouded mind and thought I had it locked up and in the bag. Sadly, I got taken down, and I thought I was done. Fortunately, I had time to correct it, and I came out victorious, but it could have turned out totally different."

"But it didn't."

"What is your reason for fighting? Why do you want to do this?" Flint prodded Steel.

"The same reason as everyone, I guess. I want the money and the clout. I want to do something more with my life than getting into trouble all the time."

"If you don't fight for something more than the money, you will not prepare properly. So, I will tell you from my experience you need to fight for a reason other than the money. Money comes and goes. When I got here, I was so full of anger and hurt. I lost my sister, and she was my entire world, but they gave me a reason to succeed, and I pushed myself. I let them push me beyond my limits. Fight for what you believe in instead of chasing a dollar. Be truthful to yourself, and you will be just fine, kid."

He stood up to walk out and turned back and gave him some dap.

"You will be fine. We got you as long as you are ready to give it your all."

Chapter Eight

BRONX

A few days later, when he was leaving the gym, Bronx ran into Steel. The guys got to talking about the fact that he had a fight coming up soon. The date wasn't set in stone because they were looking to boost ticket sales. Bronx offered to take Steel out to grab a bite and get some drinks to celebrate. Steel agreed to dinner, but no drinks. He said he had to buckle down on his training more now than ever. The pair left the gym and walked over to the sports bar across the street. They both had a taste for some wings.

"I can't hang out too late tonight. I'm putting myself on a curfew," Steel told the disappointed Bronx. "Once the fight is over, or I get into a routine, we will be able to hang out more. I just cannot afford to mess this up. I want this fight more than anything."

They were seated within moments of arriving, and their wings were brought to the table in ten minutes. Steel ordered garlic parmesan, while Bronx ordered honey barbecue. Before digging in, they each offered the other a few of their wings. Steel smiled to himself. He looked up just in time to catch Bronx smiling as well as he reached for two of Steel's wings and delivering two of his own. They ate with minimal conversation except about training and the upcoming fight. During this time, they both felt a little tension, but neither addressed it. After a few moments of silence, Bronx sparked up conversation.

"Are you ready for this fight you are begging for?" Bronx broke in between, cleaning the meat from the bones of one of his wings.

"Not yet, but I will be. I got to be. This is something I have wanted since before I walked into this place. Besides, it will let me know if I truly belong here," Steel answered him as he used his napkin to get the sauce from his hands and out from under his nails.

How is he making cleaning sauce from his fingers look so desirable?

Steel, as if he knew he was being watched, he licked the rest of the sauce from his fingers.

Damn, Bronx squirmed in his seat. To play it off,

he pretended something had bitten him on the leg, so he smacked it. A little too hard, as he then winced with pain. The more he talked and listened to Steel, the more Bronx wanted no part in getting him hurt. But how do you make a choice between family and someone you barely know?

The pair continued their meal for a few more minutes, and Steel asked for the check. But when the server brought it to them, Bronx reached for it while Steel extended his hand. Bronx grabbed it quickly, almost snatching it.

"My apologies," he said to her. She walked away with a puzzled look on her face.

"I got it this time man; you can get it next time if you like." Bronx pulled out his card and motioned with a flick of his fingers for the waitress to come back.

The waitress walked back toward them with an extra sway in her hips. Bronx noticed right away, and instinctively he looked to see if Steel seemed to have noticed. A rush of relief washed over him as it appeared to not have garnered his attention. Bronx was still trying to figure out just what or who Steel was in to. Steel was not making it easy for him.

The guys walked out together, got into Bronx's Camry, and had a silent ride back to the gym. When they arrived, Steel got out as Bronx was rolling down the passenger side window. Steel turned and bent his head down and stuck it through the window.

"Thanks, bro. I appreciate your treating tonight, and thanks for listening to me talking about the fight. I will be back to my usual self once the fight is over," tapping his hand on the roof of the car, he turned and left.

Bronx sat and watched him get to his vehicle before driving off. Everything about Steel told him he was a good guy and didn't deserve whatever Spyder was after.

After driving around, the city for an hour or so, Bronx decided to get a room. He wanted to keep the drama away from home as much as possible, especially since he was still deciding what to do. Bronx believed that if he were not at home, they wouldn't harm his mother or sister.

Over the next few days, he was still tossing around whether to give up the information he had gathered on Steel. Bronx felt it was time to go home. He had all but forgotten about his face until his sister screamed as she ran towards him.

"What happened? Who did this to you?" Deep down, she knew Spyder's goons were to blame. She hadn't wanted to see it before. She was in love and had his child. He couldn't be this horrible person everyone else made him out to be, could he?

"Oh, so you don't know who did this?" Bronx asked, but then he quickly went silent. He didn't want to involve his momma in the conversation. He had just noticed her walking into the hallway.

"My boy is home," she said, as she looked him up and down as if assessing him. Sure enough, she was. "What is going on? You are too thin, and what has happened to your face?"

"Momma, remember I told you I was working out at the gym, right? Sometimes we get a little rougher than we probably should, but it is all part of learning the craft. It isn't good enough to just give out punches. You have to be able to take them too." Bronx was able to narrowly squeeze his way out of that. His mom nodded as he was talking, as if agreeing with him. Bronx knew his mom though, she never let things go so easily. At this moment, he was grateful that she didn't protest too much. Carla, on the other hand, was determined to give him the business. As he hugged their mother and moved past her to his room, Carla marched in right behind him, quietly closing the door behind her.

"What in the world? Seriously Bronx, this is all because you're trying to leave the gang, isn't it? Why not just stay? I will beg and plead for Spyder to stay off your back. I don't want to keep seeing you this way. It will only get worse. Trust me, I've seen it."

"You have no idea that I'm doing this for you, just as much as myself. I've seen him put his hands on you, and I know I can't take him on alone. So, it is easier for us to be free of him and the gang. If I were to run, he would only resort to hurting you or Momma or worse, and I would get beat up every day before I allow that to happen. This is for you. For your freedom as much as it is mine."

Bronx heard the knock on the front door and pushed past Carla to get to it before his mom went for it.

"Momma, I got it. You rest. I'm going to step outside for a few," he said as she was getting up to answer it. He already knew it was somebody from the gang.

Charlie was waiting for him when he opened the door, leaning up against the side of the building. He had a few other goons with him. Bronx never saw him alone these days. If he ever caught Charlie slipping, he might take his chances with him.

"What gives Charlie? I have been in the house for 5 minutes. So, we are keeping tabs on me now?"

"Yeah, apparently, we are. But screw all of that. What do you have for us to take back to Spyder? His patience is wearing really thin with you these days," Charlie stated as he played with a toothpick he had in his mouth. "He pretty much gave us the go ahead to terminate your commitment to the gang, the old-fashioned way," as he tapped the 9mm that was stuck in his waistband.

Bronx had begun pacing up, and down the steps that led to his family's apartment. What should he do? Carla peeked out of the living room window at him. The look in her eyes was enough to push him to the edge. He had vowed to always protect her. Besides, would anyone blame him? Family comes first, right?

Charlie caught him looking towards the window. He motioned for her to come outside. When he sensed the hesitation, he patted his hip area, and soon the door was opening, and Carla emerged.

"Just the person I was looking for, Spyder, asked me to give something to you. Come here. I promise I won't bite."

"Carla, stay back. Go back into the house. Now!" Bronx pleaded.

She did not listen. Instead, Carla walked closer to Charlie, and he put his hand out for her hand. When she gave it to him, he quickly broke her finger. Bronx heard the snap long before she screamed out. Carla snatched her hand back and spit at Charlie, barely missing his face. Bronx ran to get between the two of them. He knew Charlie could be a jerk and do more to her.

"Look, she had nothing to do with this. You did not have to do that. I was going to tell you what I know. Trust me, one day, you are going to get yours, Charlie."

"So spit it out, little man," Charlie taunted.

"You go back and tell Spyder, Steel will have a fight soon. There is no date set just yet, but I'm sure you will know when I do. I believe we are more than done here."

"Yeah, we are done for now."

Bronx ushered his sister into the house. Momma was watching her favorite tv program, so she had not heard any of the commotions. Bronx took her to his room to be as far from their mother as he could.

"Do you want to go to the hospital?" Bronx asked, knowing she was not going for that. You have to just reset it, Bronx. Just like before."

Bronx took a deep breath as his sister did too, and with a quick movement, he heard her moan as he worked his magic on her pinky.

"Ouch," she quietly gasped. She knew it was a small price to pay. She could not go to the hospital. There would be too many questions. Carla tried that early in the relationship. The hospital called the police the second and third time she decided to go to the hospital. That was the attention she could not afford to bring to her family right now.

"What gives Bronx? Why do they want information on that guy? What are they planning?"

Bronx wanted to keep Carla out of all the drama as much as possible.

"I really don't know what their end game is. All I know is they told me to find out any and everything I could. My guess is that he is trying to break free from their hold as well. Spyder does not seem to like that very much. It would appear he has separation anxiety."

Bronx tried to sound confident in his answer so his sister would feel a little at ease and keep her nose out of his business. Trying to read her expression, it was kind of blank. He was not too sure if she believed him or not, but her questions stopped just as quickly as her few tears had.

"You do know they will be back, right? No matter what you give them, it will never be enough."

"It will have to be enough. I'm going to tell Spyder that we are done. I just need to know that you are with me. I need him to not try to come after Momma or you. That is the only reason I'm still providing him with information. If I knew you two would be safe, I'd call the police on them, but you know how that works. They would be released in a day or two, and I cannot put you or Momma at risk. So, let me handle it my way. Hopefully, it will not be too much longer. Promise me you will stay away from them, though."

Carla nodded her agreement and hugged her brother tightly. She prayed that this would all work out, but she knew she could not take anything for granted. She knew how the 5tres worked and operated. They had no conscience. Just like today, Charlie breaking her finger was for what? Bronx was willing to tell them what he had. She hated that her brother was going through the bulk of this because of her. She made a bad choice in hooking up with Spyder, but she loved him, despite everything he's done. Carla knew the relationship was not good, and she did not want to raise her child in that environment.

"Snap out of it, sis. I got you."

Bronx was exhausted. He took his shower and was getting ready for bed. His thoughts carried him to a different time and place. Thoughts of Steel had been creeping more and more into his head before bed almost nightly. His thoughts teetered back and forth between if he was doing the right thing or what if it was a different time? He and Steel could actually get to know each other without any hidden agendas. He was not too sure if Steel was chill with him because of a connection or if he somehow knew him from the gang and was trying to see what information he could get. Each night the results were the same. He would finally drift off to sleep, but his mind would be in complete chaos. Tonight, was no different.

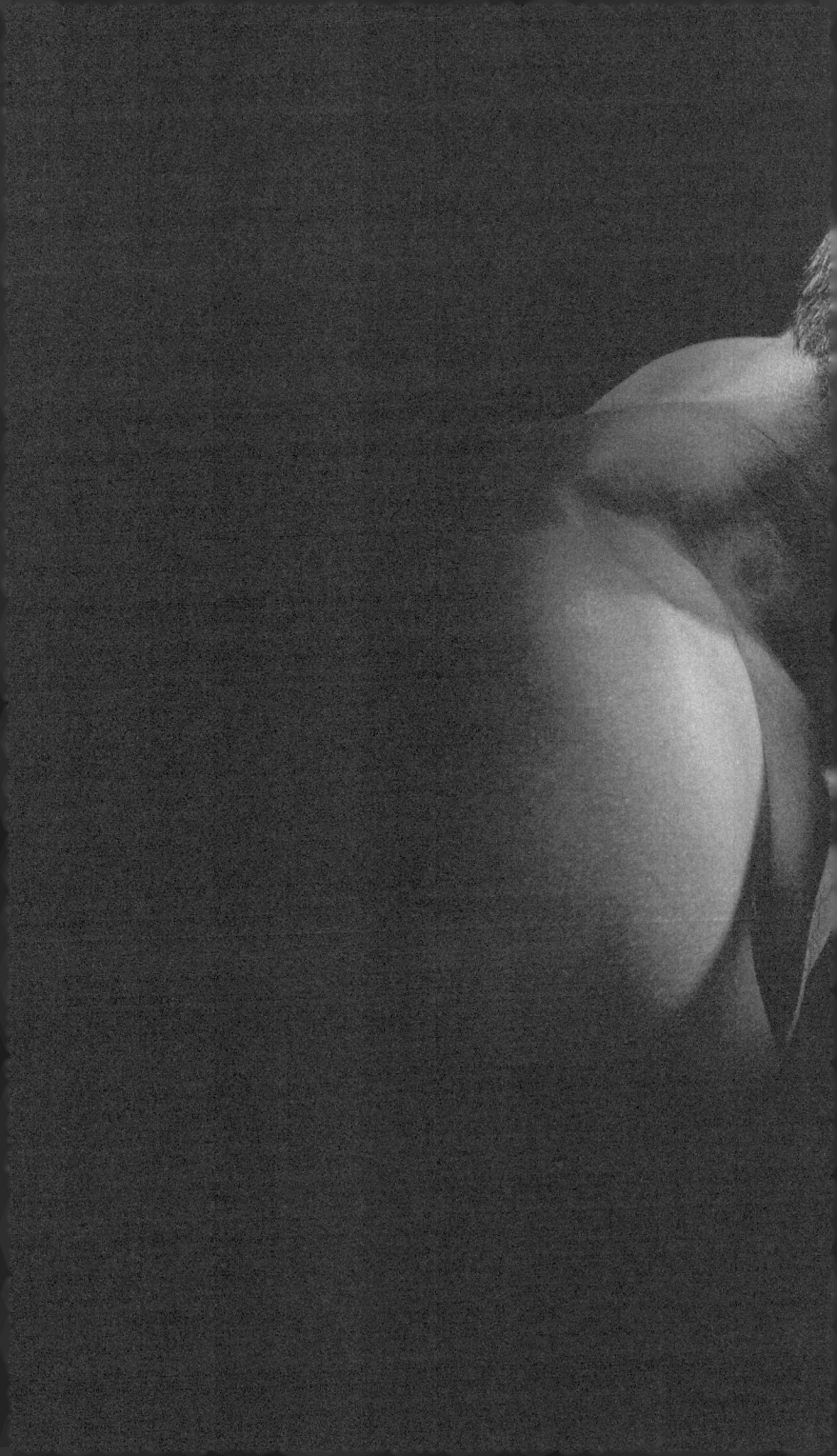

Chapter Nine

STEEL

Since Stone told Steel about the upcoming match, he had been training with more vigor than Stone had seen, even when it came to Flint. Stone felt like his gym was finally coming together again. Steel had been working so hard for a few reasons at this point. He needed to prove he was done with the life; he was prepared to buy his way out if he won the match. Thoughts of Bronx kept entering his mind, and Steel couldn't figure it out. There was an attraction, and that was something he was not used to. Although he could feel the looks of guys from time to time in the past, being his naïve self, he just thought they were looking at him because of his body. That is, from the standpoint of being envious. Steel was in amazing shape, from his legs on up to his abs and arms. Who would not want to be with him or be him? A few years back, he had tossed around the idea of allowing himself to be open to experiences with whomever, but in the world of MMA, he did not want to be viewed a certain way or viewed as being weak. There was assuredly something with Bronx. Perhaps it was how Bronx seemed to listen and make him feel like he could just be himself. Shrugging it off, he pulled out his phone to text Flint to see if they were still on for their training session. Flint responded back with a yes, and he was on his way.

While waiting on Flint, Steel decided to take an ice bath. Hoping that would relax his mind enough to regain his focus. For the last few days, he had avoided being around Bronx, especially when it could have just been the two of them. Steel had so many mixed feelings, and he had so much going on, he didn't want to lose his focus.

However, his focus was lost when he managed to drift off into a daydream, and the main visitor was Bronx. What he saw, it was so clear if he didn't know better, would have sworn it was real...

Steel opened his eyes when he heard the door close and smelled Bronx's unmistakable cologne, Mercedes. His heart began to race as he could hear the footsteps draw near. That was when he heard Bronx speaking to him.

"Hey, man. Haven't seen you much."

"Oh hey, just been busy training, you know," Steel smiled.

A smile crept to Steel's face as he watched Bronx close the distance from the door to the tub. Within seconds, he was standing beside the tub, looking down upon him. Normally Steel would feel a little tense or move to ensure he was covered but didn't move this time. Instead, Steel watched Bronx's eyes as they examined every piece of him visible beneath the ice. He smiled as his eyes spotted the tip of Steel's cock peering up between the ice cubes. Bronx made his way up until their eyes connected, and no words were said or needed. Bending down, he covered Steel's mouth with his own.

"Ummm," Steel uttered.

Bronx exuded confidence that he had never before witnessed, lifting his mouth from Steel's long enough to pull the shirt over his head. His right hand made a trail down the length of Steel's chest and abdomen until it reached his cock. Gently, he teased the tip with his middle finger, making slow circles. Bronx smiled as he could feel and hear the water shift. He smiled even deeper as Steel shifted underneath the ice. He wanted Bronx to feel the fullness in the palm of his hand. Pushing up through the ice, Steel's cock was rock hard, cold, and throbbing. It quickly warmed against Bronx's hand as he began to massage up and down, slowly at first, never taking his eyes off Steel's. It was important to Steel that Bronx knew he was okay with this happening. He showed him this by thrusting his hips up and down to get him to quicken his pace. Bronx got the hint and began jerking faster. When he felt Steel was ready to explode, he again covered his mouth with his and sucked on Steel's tongue until he released it all over his hand. Bronx gently pushed down on Steel's cock so the water could cover it. He stood, and as quickly as he came, grabbed his shirt, and began to walk out, never stopping to look back, closing the door gently behind him.

{{{{Knock-Knock}}}}

Steel shifted, jolted from his daydream at the sudden noise.

"Aye, bro, you in there?" Flint asked as he pushed open the door.

"Umm yeah yeah.... I'm here. Just finishing up an ice bath. Thought it would relax me. Turns out it did. Hey, did you happen to see anyone out there before you came in?"

"Nah, bro. Just me. Why, what's going on?"

"I guess nothing. Thought I heard something a few moments ago. Probably just my imagination, and then there was you."

"You ready to train or what, man? Jade told me I couldn't hang out too late today," he said with a grin on his face.

"Yeah, bro, I appreciate you coming. I promise we will not be long. I would hate to get on Jade's wrong side. I've seen what she does to people on her bad side. Give me a moment to get cleaned up, and I will be out there by the time you get warmed up."

Flint turned to head back out the door as Steel stood up to get out of the tub. Usually, he was not ashamed of his manhood, but for some reason, today, he felt a little embarrassed at the fact he was standing at attention in a cold bath. He would have never lived it down if Flint had seen it.

Steel took a quick bird shower to warm up a little bit before throwing on his boxer briefs, shorts, and his tank top with the gym's logo. The Phoenix represented him all too well. That might be why he loved it here.

"Aye, bro," Flint yelled out as he watched Steel coming through the door to the gym. "You not going to believe me, man but, the wifey called. I have been summoned. She said Hannah isn't acting right. Would love to stay, but I got to go."

"Oh yeah, man. Go, trust me, I understand. Family matters, above all else. I hope everything is good."

Grabbing his workout bag from the corner of the ring, he was out the door in seconds. Only stopping briefly to call over his left shoulder, "I'll call you, bro."

Just as Steel turned to walk over to the punching bag, he hears Bronx talking with a few other guys who had just come in with him. The last few days, he seemed to have avoided Bronx, and he was getting good at it, but he could not do it forever. Today proved it. Bronx walked toward him after ending his conversation with the guys.

"Hey Steel, wait up," he said, jogging up to Steel. Although he wanted to keep walking to avoid Bronx, he turned and stopped, waiting for him to close in.

"What's up?"

"I haven't seen you around in a few days, or not much should I say."

"Yeah, I've just been focused. I am just trying to get as much training done as possible to show Stone that I am taking this opportunity seriously. He has done a lot for me since I've been here."

Bronx's demeanor changed after a few moments into their chat. Steel couldn't put his fingers on it, but something was going on with Bronx. His confidence level seemed off, and he appeared nervous.

"Hey bro, what's going on with you? Anything we

need to talk about," he noticed that Bronx turned and looked away.

"I'm cool. Just...I've got a lot on my mind these days. No need to bother anyone else with my issues, you know."

"You do know that you can always talk to me, right?" Steel paused for effect before he continued, "I know I've been preoccupied, but I'm always here if you need a friend."

"Well, if you have a few minutes, I would like to get your advice on something. But only if you have time."

"Of course, I do. It seems you are in luck. My sparring partner just bailed on me. So what's up? What is eating away at you?"

"Can we go outside to talk and get some fresh air?"

Steel nodded and started walking towards the back door. He thought it would be less of a crowd if they went out back. He led the way to a bench that was set up for just such occasions. Using his hand, he wiped the bench off, and he sat, followed directly by Bronx.

"A'ight man, let's have it. Seriously, what's going on?"

Bronx let out a long sigh. How could he tell this

man his whole reason for being here without getting knocked out?

"Listen, there is no easy way for me to say this. I care about you and your wellbeing," Bronx leans over and kisses Steel full on the lips.

Chapter Ten

STEEL

"What gives man?" Steel could not believe what had just happened as he backed off from Bronx. Sure, he had thought about things, but never had he acted on it. Wait, was he giving off a gay vibe? His mind started retracing and replaying previous interactions.

"Bro, I am so sorry. I did not mean it." Bronx paused. "Actually, that is not true. I did mean it, but I did not mean to offend you. I thought I read that you would be okay. Now I just feel foolish."

"Dude, that was not cool. Not at all." Steel turned and walked back in the direction of the gym. Still in disbelief about what had just transpired. He needed to clear his head.

Bronx hated himself right now. How did I read him wrong? Maybe it is just me. Looking for something in the wrong place. Get it together, Bronx. After a few more moments of self-loathing, he decided it was best to head anywhere but to the gym. The crazy part is what he really wanted to tell Steel he did not. He began to walk towards his ride.

"Hey, if it isn't my main man Bronx. How are you doing, buddy?" Charlie said with a smile on his face. He was with a few other lower-level thugs that ran with the 5tres.

"Come on. You cannot be serious, Charlie. I have not had time to get anything new."

Charlie lets out a laugh deep in his gut. "Yeah, I guess not. You were too busy doing other things," he said, pulling out his phone, flipping through his picture gallery.

"What are you talking about?"

Charlie turned his phone around so Bronx could see the picture of him kissing Steel. "You are a disgusting creature. There were rumors, but I had not actually seen you until today. That single act turned my stomach."

The guys that were with him agreed with him. Bronx noticed they started walking in closer to him, even as he was backing away.

"Listen, guys, I don't want any problems. You had no right to take pictures of me. That is a violation," is all he got out of his mouth before he felt the first of many punches. This was becoming the norm, and he did not like it.

"You guys think you're so tough when you are jumping me. How about one-on-one? Let us see how tough you are," he managed to get out in between the assault.

"You have to know we will get our way. You can keep being our punching bag if you like. It will not stop the result. However, since you are not cooperating and you should, maybe we should visit your family. What do you think about that?" Charlie spoke.

Struggling to stand up, Bronx spoke out, "You can't get to him. I have tried. You have done enough to my family. Hurt me all you want. They have done nothing to deserve it."

"You just gave us our way to get to him. I have already sent the picture to Spyder, and he told me to use it if necessary. We do not want to hurt anyone else, but what Spyder wants, Spyder gets. This guy has something, and the boss wants it. So, I guess maybe you are off the hook. I am not sure yet. We will be in touch."

The guys pushed Bronx around a bit more before walking away from him as he fell to the ground.

"Man, could this day get any worse?"

Two men grabbed him and dragged him into their van.

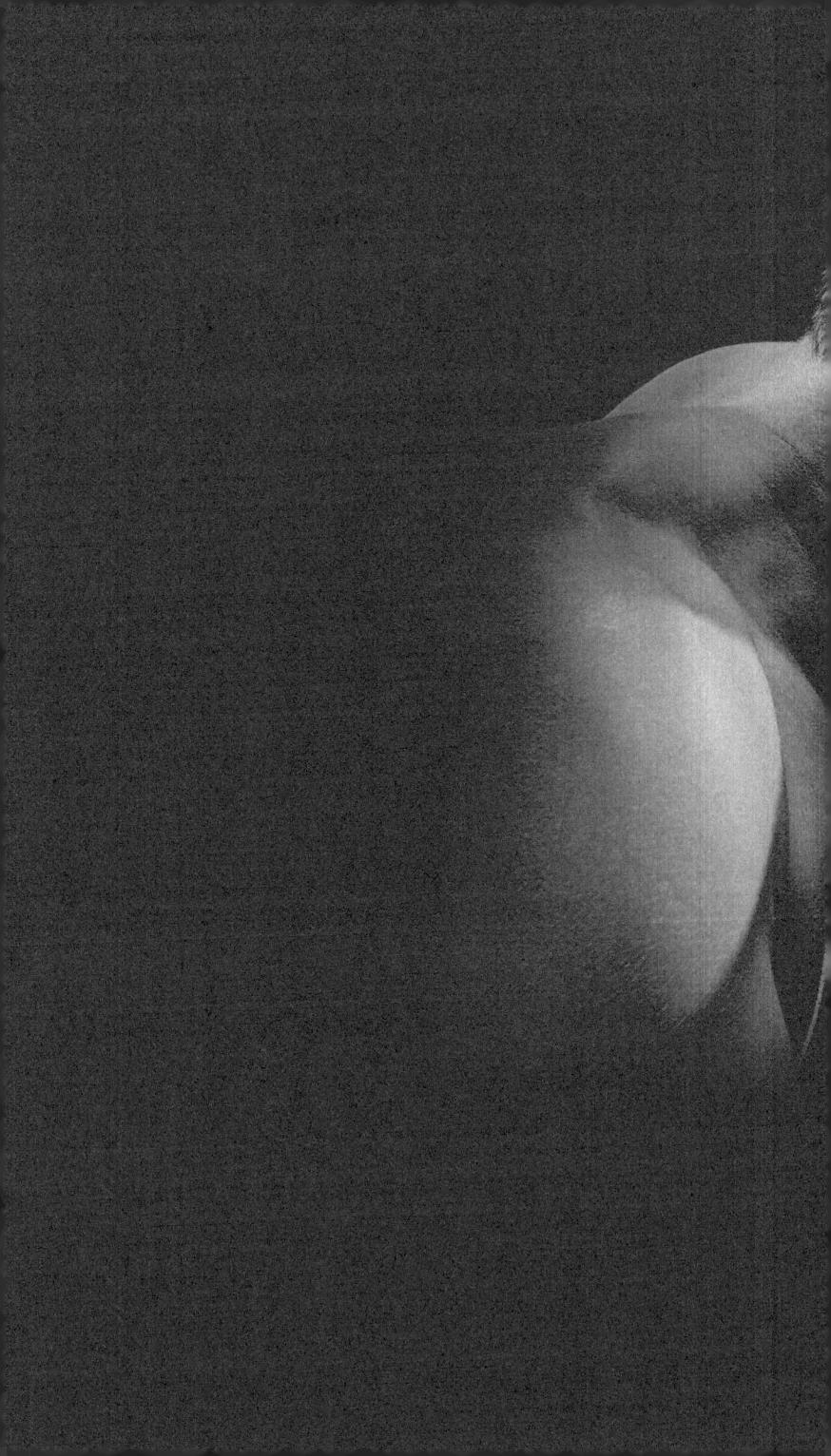

Chapter Eleven

STEEL

B ack inside the gym, Steel's mind was all over the place. The events of the previous hour were invading his mind. He was working out with the punching bag; he really could have used Flint about now.

Even if he thought I was into that, what right did he have to just take it upon himself to do that? He is lucky I did not punch his lights out. He is a nice guy, and I did have thoughts, but damn it, he just had no right. What if someone saw him? What if I am attracted to him? Would it be the end of the world?

"Hey Steel, my man. You seem like a man on a mission. Is everything cool," Stone asked as he walked up and saw a look of distress on Steel's face.

"Man, you wouldn't believe me even if I told you." He stopped focusing on the punching bag, looking Stone's way.

"Go ahead and try me. It is bothering you, so what can it hurt? It may help you. I mean, that is what we are here for. You know to help," he said, smiling.

"I just feel as if there is about to be some drama in some form or another. I have an uneasy feeling. Do you always know when you are attracted to someone? Yeah, I know that kind of sounds childish, but I'm being serious. Have you ever had someone invade your space?"

"I honestly have not had anyone to be that bold. I can imagine it would give you cause to pause and think for a moment. Is this someone you value? Do you, in fact, have feelings towards them?"

Steel shrugged his shoulders. He could not rightfully answer those questions. "I appreciate you listening," Steel said, running his hand through his hair. That was the thing he did when he was frustrated. "I guess I just have to figure some stuff out. Thanks again Bro, I think I'm going to go work out a little more."

Steel took off his gloves and walked over to the weights. He thought maybe lifting a bit would ease his mind. It did not work. He just could not seem to focus. Just then, his phone buzzed in his pocket, he checked it, and there was a message from Flint. He was apologizing for not being able to make it back to work out. Flint did promise that if everything went well, he would catch up with him sometime tomorrow. Steel sent back a quick text saying no worries, and before he could put his phone back away, it was vibrating. This time there was a call from an unknown number. Something seemed familiar about it, though. So, he answered.

"Hello,"

"It's been a while, my friend. It seems as if you have forgotten about your brothers," It was Spyder's voice that greeted him.

"Friend, huh? Is that what we are calling it these days," Steel shot back.

"If I were you, I would stick with friend. Ohhhh, that reminds me, I have a friend who would love to see you."

Steel was confused for a moment. He did not know of anyone being affiliated with the gang, especially that he would call a friend. How wrong he was.

"You got quiet on me, bro. You, okay?" Spyder did not wait for his response. "You should really come and hang out with us for a bit. We miss you terribly," he said sarcastically.

"I am no longer a part of your family. I don't want anything to do with you guys."

"That is just it. You can't just walk away from us. At least without giving us something. So, are you going to come to visit us? I mean, I am asking nicely," Spyder urged.

"You aren't hearing me, bro. I'm done with that life."

"Well, that hurts my heart. You see, I happened upon this picture that I would like to share with you. I did not want to take it public, but if you prefer. It stars you and Bronx. Yeah, he is here right now, and he don't look so good, bro."

"Don't hurt him. I'll be there soon," Steel said as he hung up his phone.

Steel could not believe what was happening. He looked around for Stone but did not see him as he gathered his belongings and headed towards the door. His mind was spinning.

Chapter Twelve

BRONX

I had to ask if things could get any worse. Now I have my answer. Bronx had been knocked out when the guys brought him back to their spot. When his father Carlos had died from a heart attack, things around the house began to get tight. His father only had enough insurance money to cover his burial and his mother's plot. The bills were beginning to pile up, and even though Bronx was only a teen at the time, he had to find a way to step it up.

It was so easy getting initiated into the gang. Robbing someone that is easy. He wanted to be a part of the gang life so badly. Everyone he knew was a part of the 5tres and had been for life. Back in the day, the gang helped each other out. If someone were behind on their bills, they would go away. Bronx did not know that the people collecting the bills were being threatened or hurt. He, as a kid, knew his mom was not coming home crying every day after working from sunup to sundown.

Opening his eyes, he realized he missed his papa. If Carlos were alive to see him now, he would not approve. He had always been against the gangs, and he often stood up against the gangbangers that threatened his neighborhood. Thinking about it now, that was possibly one of the appeals with getting Bronx to join the gang. It was all too easy.

He overhead Spyder on the phone. He knew it was Steel. As soon as Spyder hung up, he turned to his gang and laughed about how he had just punked Steel into coming in.

"These cats think they are so smart. One day, they will learn that they can't beat fate," Spyder smiled as he spoke.

"He is coming in?" Charlie asked.

"Oh yeah. He is coming okay. I almost feel bad for him. He cares too much about what people think about him. You know me. I am who and what I am. I do not make excuses for it. You do not like it. So, what? Move on. But not him, and not this piece of trash in the other room." Spyder walked around the partition to look at Bronx. "He seems to care about you and your secret," he said as he kicked Bronx in the gut.

Bronx let out a muffled moan in pain; he couldn't talk if he wanted to. They had his mouth taped shut. Spyder bent down to lean over him and punched him in his right temple, knocking him out cold.

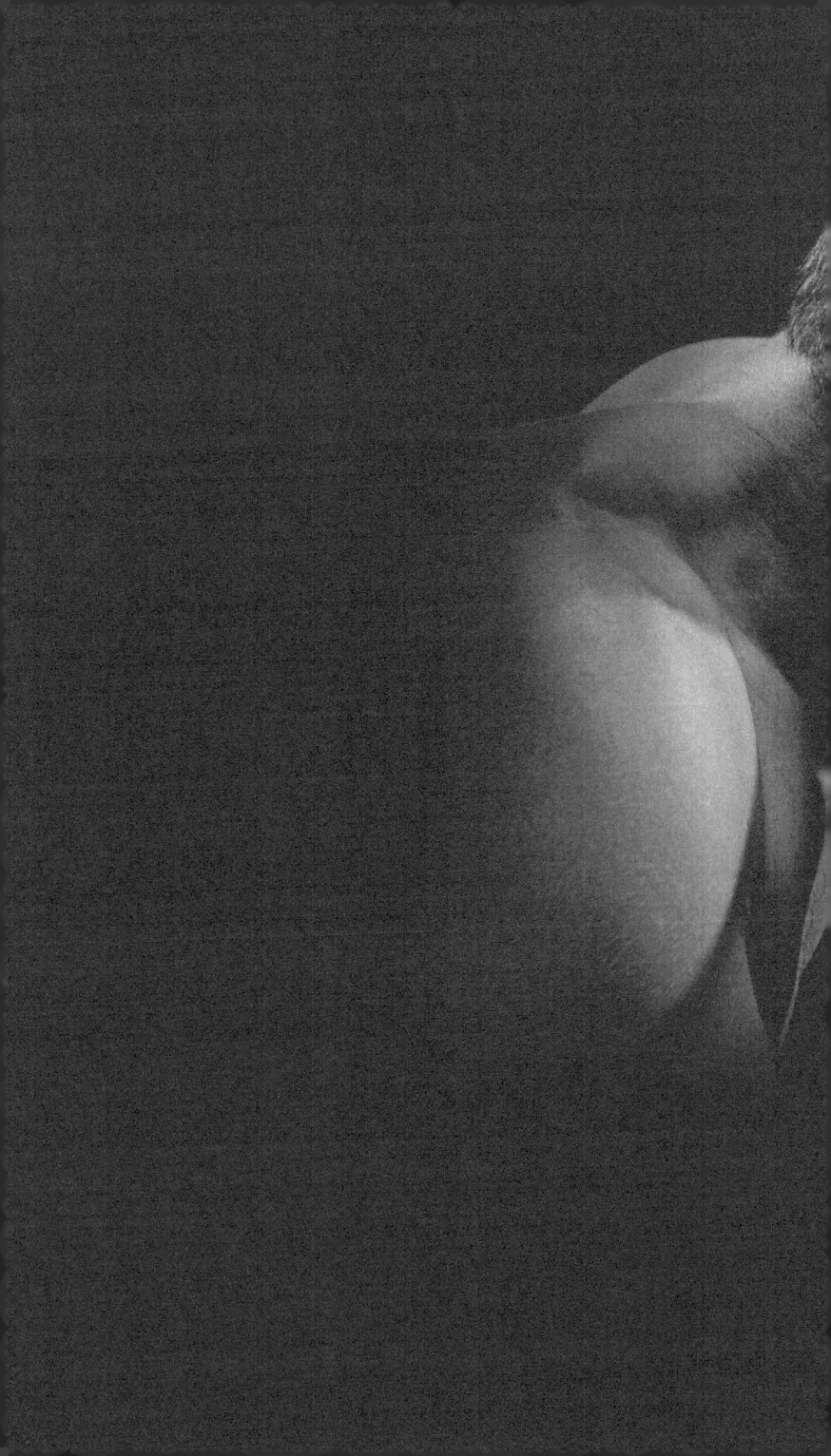

Chapter Thirteen

STEEL

So much was going through his mind. In an instant, his world was being turned upside down. Nothing at this point should surprise him. Steel developed an uneasy feeling the closer he got to his destination. If someone had told him that his world would be in shambles today, he would never have believed it. No matter how much he tried to clear his thoughts, they kept relapsing to the worst scenario. His career would be over before it began.

Steel looked down at his phone to verify the address as he pulled in the entrance to The Towers, one of Spyder's newly acquired properties. The further he drove into the gated area; he knew he was in the right place. He could see several of Spyder's goons lurking about. Charlie walked out to meet him when he noticed the vehicle approaching.

"Hey, my main man. What's been up? I haven't seen you lately," Charlie teased.

"Come on now, Charlie, you and I, we were never cool, bro. You always thought I wanted your spot. I was just a kid trying to fit in. That is until I learned better. I knew this life was not for me."

"Oh, but it was good enough to get you some good money. That is, until you decided that it was no longer good enough." He said, mocking Steel.

"You think you can make me feel bad for wanting more than this?" Steel turned with his arms outstretched. "I was trying to leave this world behind, but somehow, someway, you keep pulling me back. Let's go! Let's go see the great and powerful Spyder," he said with frustration.

"I almost feel bad for you, bro." Charlie said as he turned towards the house.

Steel noticed that Charlie did not take him through the front entrance, but he opted to use the side door. Once inside, Steel understood why. Directly across the room, he spotted Bronx. He was curled up into a fetal position. Steel noticed he wasn't moving. He stared long enough to see his chest move up and down, then sighed in relief.

Steel's heart went out to him. The ones who did this went too far.

Spyder walked into the room, looked over in

Bronx's direction. The smile that was on his face made Steel's gut turn.

"It is a shame what happened to him, eh?"

"Is it, man? Or was it overkill? Everyone knows your generals don't make moves without your consent. That is one thing I know and learned well during my time here."

"Yeah, about that whole leaving the family thing. Why didn't you just come to me? We could have discussed it like men."

"You would have never just let me walk. You are not a negotiating type of guy. At least that's what I've been told."

"I guess we will never know. One thing I can assure you of is that I am a businessman, and because of this, I see an opportunity for us to make a deal."

"I'll bite. What is your deal?"

"Something recently fell into my lap, and it would be irresponsible of me to not make you aware of it. You know, to see if we can figure a way to make this negative thing into a win for us all," Spyder paused, looking as if he were truly concerned about Steel's well-being. He sold it with his hand under his chin and a puzzled look.

Steel felt as if he was prolonging the information to keep him focused on the fact that Bronx still had not woken up. Steel was not amused at all, but he knew that it could make things worse if he was blatantly disrespectful. So, he stood there and listened. Steel looked down at his watch.

"Oh, my apologies. I'm sure that you must have somewhere else to be. Far be it from me to hold you up."

"It is just a habit. I'm here. I came, didn't I?"

Giggling, "Yeah-yeah, you did. Well, let me get to it. It is really simple. A picture was sent to me. By now, I'm sure you can guess what it was of, right?" Spyder asked while he pulled out his phone and scrolled through his pictures, stopping at the one Charlie had forwarded to him earlier. Holding his phone out to Steel to take it and look. He did, and his heart dropped. The kiss had lasted no more than a few seconds, but apparently, that is all it took to snap the photo. Steel gave the phone back to Spyder.

"What's your deal, man?"

"You don't want to deny that picture? I'm sure you wish you could, but anyway, since a picture is worth a thousand words, I wonder how it equates to dollars."

Steel wasn't quite understanding. "You want me to pay you for that picture? Dude, if that is the case, I'm not hustling anymore, and even when I was, I was no good."

"You are correct. You were terrible at it," he said

while laughing. "What I want? I heard you're fighting now. You've been hanging out at the gym, getting all buffed up and shit. I need for you to make sure that in your upcoming fight, which is your first, right? I need you to make sure you don't win. The fight is a few days away, so until then, we will sit on your buddy and the photo," Spyder looks over at Bronx, who begins to stir a bit.

Steel shook his head. He could not believe what was happening. "Man, if I knew you were going to have your foot on my neck, I guess I should have just stayed in the gang. If I do this, and I mean if you leave him alone as well, and that includes families, I remember how you guys roll," Steel said as his mind began to turn.

"You have my word. He has more than served his purpose to us at this point. And from one man to another, I can appreciate the loyalty you have for him. I just hope he had the same for you," Spyder walked closer toward Steel and reached out for his hand.

Steel did not take it. Instead, he offered up his acceptance of the deal. Steel was always a man of his word, so he didn't want to shake on the deal because that meant it was a closed case. As he walked over and knelt down to where Bronx lay, he called back over his shoulder to Spyder, "Unless something changes, OK?"

"It is going to be okay," he whispered to Bronx, who was too numb to acknowledge his presence. Patting him on the back, he stood up and made his way out of the house. When he got to the door, he called back in, "Can you at least make him comfortable?" Spyder shook his head in agreement.

Steel made his way back to his car and headed toward the gym. He carefully slid his phone from his pocket and dialed Stone's number. Surprisingly, Stone answered on the first ring.

"Aye, Bro, what's up? They told me you bolted out of here like a bat out of hell."

"I need your help."

"Do you need me to come to you, or are you headed back to the gym?" Stone asked aggressively.

"I am heading to you. I'm sorry, man. I'll see you soon." Steel pressed the end call button.

಄

STONE WAITED IN THE OFFICE UNTIL STEEL arrived. He watched through the window as Brick, another brother of his, executed his workout in preparation for his fight coming up. Steel walked in the door, interrupting his thoughts. Stone noticed he was out of sorts. He tried to give him time to calm down before he started questioning him.

"Before you get started, remember I told you we are here for you. There isn't anything we can't fix. So just breathe and talk, okay?"

Steel nodded his head. "So many things that could go wrong, and they did, man. I don't even know truthfully where to begin."

"Slow down, start from the beginning. Your beginning."

"Remember, I told you about the 5tres, right?"

"Yeah, you thought someone may have been following you. Is there more?"

"There is more," Steel exhaled deeply. Stone motioned for him to come on out with it. "You know the guy that has been hanging around for the last bit," he waited until Stone acknowledged he did. "I thought he was just friendly, but he is the one who invaded my space." He paused again to gauge Stone's response. When he noticed no change at all, he continued. "Until today, we have hung out a few times, and he has always been full of questions, but I thought he was just being friendly. Trying to learn about the MMA thing, you know? Before I go any further, I have to admit that I have some sort of feelings about him, but before you start asking what they are, I really don't know. Nor do I know if that is even a road I want to venture down. Well, today, he wanted to talk, or at least he said he did. Long story short is he kissed me. I didn't move back right away or smack him, but it lasted a few seconds, max. Apparently, that was long enough to let someone who had been watching me take a picture."

"This may be a stupid question, but how did they know to be watching at that moment? Is it possible he was a part of the plan, or were they watching him?" Stone questioned.

"I was starting to wonder about it all. When Spyder called me to meet him, he already had Bronx. They beat him really bad. I honestly don't know what to think anymore. What I do know is they have threatened that they will release the picture and do something pretty bad to Bronx if I don't agree to do something very stupid."

"Let me guess? You don't have a lot of money, no offense. Not a lot of family. But what you do have is this fight coming up, right? So they want you to throw it, and they will bet against you to make sure they come out on top. I guess they didn't like the odds if you fight."

"I owe you so much. If I take a dive, that will make your gym look bad. I don't want to do that. Besides, we have worked so hard to prep. What's the worst that can happen if the picture gets out and my sexuality is in question," he asked with his head lowered in shame.

"Bro, listen, you are who you are. You are putting too much stress on yourself. All I care about is if you are a good man. That is all. If anybody here at the gym decided to give you grief about your personal business, let me know, and it would be me they would have to deal with. As far as the world of MMA, they do not care. They care if you can fight or not. So, shake that off you. Focus on what is important. How can I help you?"

"Tell me what I should do?"

"Even if I wanted to, I can't tell you what to do, but what I can do is do a few things on my own. No matter what you decide, know that I got your back. So, do me a favor, clear your head as much as possible, and for the next day, continue to train. The day before the fight, you will come to stay at my place so your body can fully rest, and I can keep an eye on you."

"You don't have to babysit me, bro."

"This is what I do for my guys. And you are now my Lil bro, so if this is what you want to do, I got you."

This seemed to have eased Steel's mind a bit. He was ready to head back into the gym.

"You have time to work out a bit in the ring? I

know I've held you up, but I could really use the help if you have time."

Stone nodded as the two exited the office and headed straight for the ring. They each proceeded to do some warmups to loosen themselves up. The pair worked out for hours, neither keeping track of the time.

The workout session went better than Steel imagined. He could tell there were a few moves Stone was not ready for and a few that surprised him altogether. Steel thought no more about Bronx, or Spyder, or the impending decision that would have to be made the rest of the night.

Chapter Fourteen

BRONX

The last few days, Bronx had been in and out of consciousness. He heard the deal that Spyder made with Steel, and it was not fair. How could he have been so stupid and careless? Bronx began to question himself and what he could have or should have done differently. Of course, he knew it was pointless to think about that all now. He just felt horrible.

He began to look around the room, trying to see if anything could help him somehow get free. He saw nothing. Bronx became more frustrated. He started yelling he needed to use the bathroom. He was unsure if it would work because he could not recall them letting him use it before, yet he didn't smell as if he had relieved himself. Thank God, that would have been a bit embarrassing, but somewhat understandable, given the circumstances.

One of Spyder's soldiers, Marco, comes through to do his rounds and sees what all the commotion was about.

"So glad to see you man, I need to go to the bathroom and bad," Bronx spoke up.

"I don't know dude, I was told you got no privileges," Marco said but thought about it. "Nobody deserves that, though."

Marco stood over Bronx as he lifted him up to a standing position. He walked him to the door leading outside.

"Now listen, dude, I am going to loosen the ropes so you can use your hands. I'm not with that holding onto someone else's business. No judgment, though," he said to Bronx.

"Thanks, man. I appreciate it. You think when I finish, I can get a smoke? It has been a few long days."

"You're pushing your luck now, man," another of Spyder's goons Tito, walked up and interjected himself into the conversation. "You are lucky he is letting you use the bathroom. Be thankful. Our orders were clear."

Bronx turned his back to the guys, unzipped his pants, and began to urinate into the bushes beside the house. After he had been relieving himself for what seemed like forever, a gust of wind blew and pushed his urine in the direction of Marco, who was standing downwind of him.

"Ayeeee bro, what gives?"

"Dude, it wasn't me. The wind took hold of it. I tried to control it," Bronx said unapologetically.

"Aye, Tito, watch him while I go find something else to put on. This is disgusting, man."

Marco went into the house, leaving Tito to make sure Bronx was taken back inside after he finished and secured him.

Bronx saw a slight chance for him to overpower the loudmouth youngster now in charge of him.

"How about that smoke? I mean, before I go back in and wait while my fate is being decided and all. Consider it my last request."

Tito felt a little bad for him, so he agreed, and when he reached into his jacket pocket to retrieve his Newports, Bronx made his move. He had been practicing with Steel a few of his take-down moves. Bronx spun around and kicked him in the shin, and without hesitation, Tito went down with a grunt. He was grabbing his shin as he fell over.

Bronx gathered his strength and took off running. There was a wooded area behind the housing development. He thought that would help camouflage him while he got away. The sun was going down.

All Bronx could think of was that he needed to

get to Steel before making a bad decision. After running around in the woods for a few hours, he finally made it back to familiar ground. It surprised him that no more men had come running after him. He only heard Charlie and Tito. He was not concerned about Charlie so much. He had a bad leg, so he was not very fast. Checking his pockets for his phone, he was not shocked it was not there, but he had to check. Bronx knew he could not be caught out alone. He makes his way to the gym.

As he nears Phoenix, he spots Stone about to leave. He called out to him, hoping that he would hear him out. He was almost certain that he knew part of what was going on. Stone and Steel were very close and respectful to each other. Bronx also noticed how they acted alike at times.

"Stone!"

Stone turned at the sound of his name. He turned, squinting his eyes to make out the person who was calling his name. When he recognized who it was, he walked over to where Bronx stood, hunched over. He was still in a lot of pain but was trying to push through it.

"Hey Bronx, you, okay? You are not looking so good," Stone puts his arm around Bronx and helps him into the gym through the side entrance. Stone did not want to answer questions, nor did he know just who he could trust. Once he helped Bronx inside, he went and looked out the door before locking it. He noticed a black SUV had pulled up. Stone just shook his head. He was ready. He knew he needed to hurry and get to the arena. Flint was with Steel, and the fight was due to start within the hour.

Stone was the first to speak. "Listen, dude, I don't know all the ins and outs, but what I do know is you are trouble. And to be honest, I don't like trouble. I've watched you around here, and I have never approached you because you played lowkey. I think you were sent here with bad intentions. Especially since Steel did not start seeing things or getting vibes until you showed up. Now is your time to talk, and I suggest you do it fast. I have somewhere to be."

Bronx had a serious lump in his throat. He was not expecting that from Stone, shit he didn't know what to expect, but it was not that.

"I never meant to cause any harm." He took a deep breath before proceeding. "You know the 5tres, right? I mean, everybody knows them. They have been threatening my family, and they promised to do worse if I did not help them gather information about Steel. It all started when he got released from jail. They were planning to jump him or something in there because they knew he had been ducking and dodging them. The leader Spyder did not like that." He paused to catch his breath.

"Out with it," Stone urged.

"Well, you bailed him out. Spyder asked me to watch him and try to figure out why you helped him. I could not figure that out. I told them there was nothing here. You were just doing some charity work. Then you had to go and start training him. Then there was the fight being announced. It was a dream come true for Spyder. You see, Steel was not great at the bad guy stuff, so what better way to capitalize on him, win or lose? The guy fights, they bet. Win, win is how they saw it. I did not know the full plan until they held me, and I heard them making a deal with Steel." Then it struck him. He needed to get to Steel. He could not let him throw the fight.

"I messed up. I gave them the leverage they needed. It was an accident. Well, not me kissing him." He looked at Stone to see if his demeanor had changed, and it didn't. He continued on, "I didn't know they were watching him or me like that. Spyder saw an opportunity. I need to tell Steel what happened. I need to tell him the part I played."

Stone's phone vibrated from his pocket. He reached for it and answered.

"Flint, Flint, what's up? Everything okay." He could hear a brief commotion in the background.

"Yeah, Stone, some guys just walked up in here, said they were here to support Steel, but he said they are not friendly. How do you want me to proceed?"

"You should have some company arriving any second now. You remember my guy Tony, right?" No sooner than his name was mentioned, Flint saw him coming through the doors to the locker room. He was not alone. When the guys saw Tony and his comrades coming through with their uniforms, they decided to leave.

"That's okay, we will wait outside," one called back over his shoulder as he went through the door. Spyder had sent them into the locker room to ensure that he did not develop second thoughts about the fight.

"Flint, I am on my way. There was a slight delay, but I will explain when I see you. Just make sure no one gets too close to my boy."

"You got it. See you soon," Flint said into the phone.

Steel immediately relaxed after hearing that Stone would be there soon. He was already nervous about the fight, to begin with, and when you compound that with his decision to throw it or not, it was just too much. He already threw up once since arriving at the arena. Steel saw the crowd of people and could not believe they were there to see his first fight, win or lose.

Stone made a few more phone calls as he handed his keys to Bronx for him to drive. "Hey, don't wreck my baby. You know where we go, right?"

Bronx nodded, and when they arrived at Stones truck, he got in on the driver's side. The truck fit Stone to a T. It was a big body. It was awkward for Bronx to step up into the truck, but he made it up the two steps and into the driver's seat due to him being 5ft 6inches and Stone was 6ft 4inches. Bronx thought Stone was handsome in a rugged sort of way. Not exactly what he was finding himself attracted to.

Bronx drove them across town to the arena. By the time they arrived, the fight was already in the first round. Steel was struggling, and Bronx knew it was because of him. It's like he wasn't even fighting back. He was relieved when the bell sounded, indicating round one was over. He and Stone made it to Steel's corner in time to talk some sense into him.

"Thank God you are here, Stone. I don't know what he is doing out there," Flint spoke up first.

Bronx went to Steel and whispered, "I am sorry.

Whatever you need me to do, I will do. But what I need for you to do is not let them take this from you."

Stone mouthed, "Fight," when Steel looked his way.

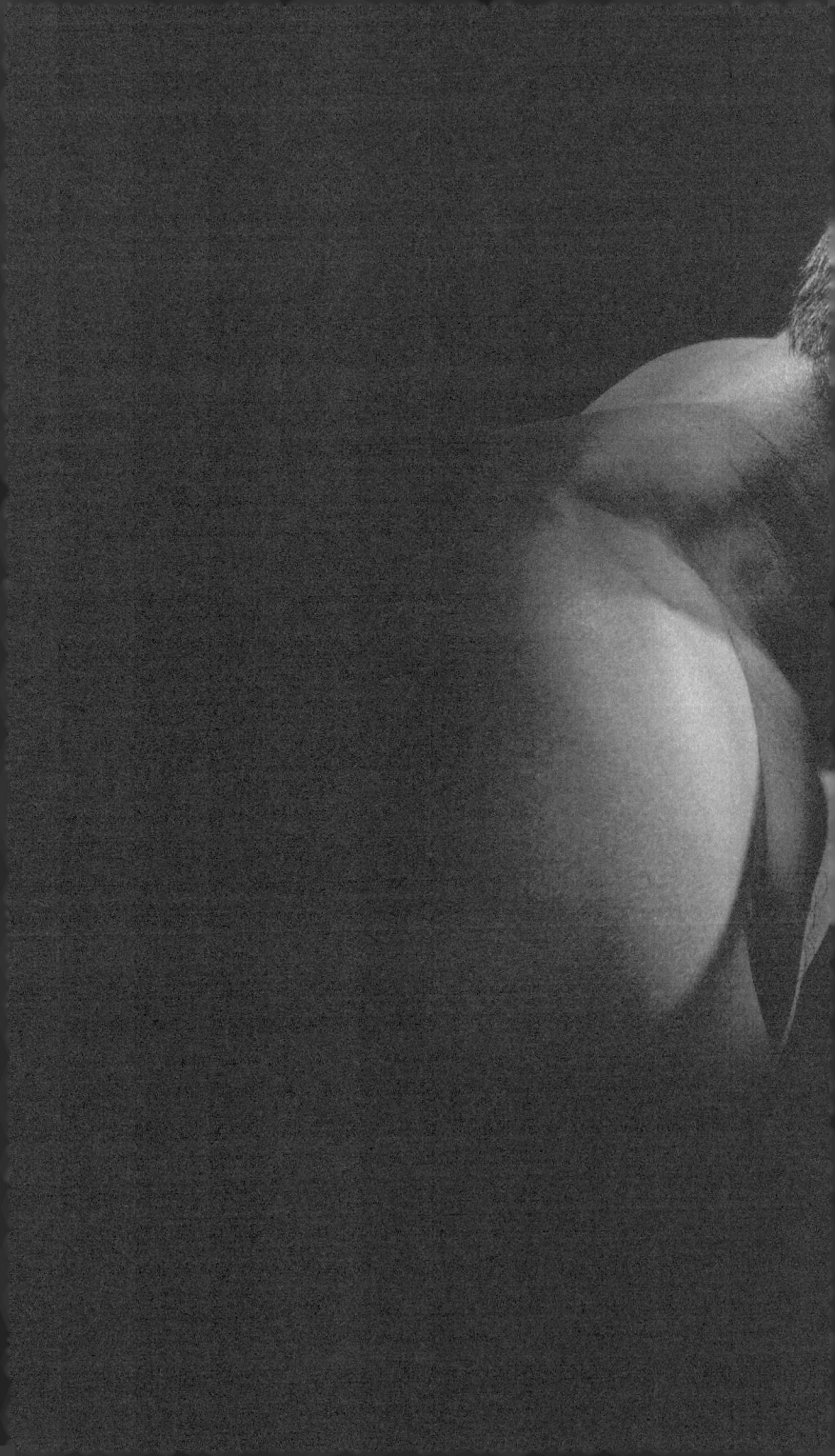

Chapter Fifteen

STEEL

The first round did not sit well with Steel. He knew it was not right to throw the match, and all he needed was that additional push from Stone to know it was okay. He owed it to himself to give this his all. Otherwise, why was he training so hard? If the pictures leaked, oh well, that he would deal with it.

The bell sounded for round two. Steel went out to the center of the mat with a whole new mindset. He went on the attack. Steel threw some jabs, only connecting on two of them. That seemed to have shaken his opponent Amir up. He fired back a combo of his own that stunned Steel for a moment.

"Get in there," Stone yelled. "Don't wait for him to come to you."

Steel did as he was instructed and let off a multitude of left and right hooks, each connecting to

Amir's head. He did not stop until Amir stumbled back and fell to the mat as the bell was sounding.

The referee checked Amir's vision and status as he made his way up to his feet. Amir shook his head that he was okay. He stumbled over to his corner. The ref walked over to the corner and asked if he wanted to continue.

"Yes, we will continue," his coach answered for him.

In Steels corner, Stone was giving him advice on moving his feet more and using his legs. Bronx was nervous as he looked around and could see a few of the 5tres throughout the arena.

The bell sounds off for round three.

Steel bounces out into the middle of the ring, remembering what Stone instructed. He was finding his footing. He danced around Amir, moving back and forth quickly, and calculated. Steel threw a right-handed jab that landed squarely on Amir's chin. He shook his head, trying to shake it off. Before he could get set to counter, another jab came, this time with more power and from the left. This one landed half an inch to the right of the last one. Taking a step back, he kicked Amir in the right thigh. Amir's leg gave out, and he went down. Steel leaned in and stuck Amir with another jab from his right. Amir fell backward. Steel could not believe it. He knocked him out.

"Hell yeah," Stone and Flint yelled out in unison.

Before the ref could call the fight because of the knockout, Stone and Flint were in the ring, raising Steel into the air. Bronx remained in the corner, but with a smile on his face. It was hard to smile through the pain he still felt, but he did. He was genuinely happy for Steel. Bronx made his way to the locker room, following slowly behind Steel, Flint, and Stone. When they were safely in the room, Stone stepped back out to answer a phone call.

"Hey, is it done?" He spoke into his phone.

"Yeah, all wrapped up. Just had a nice chat with Spyder as well. He will not be bothering anyone else for a bit. He realized Steel and Bronx were not worth his freedom. Besides, he is already down a few foot soldiers, can't afford to lose many more."

"Thank you, bro. I owe you a solid."

"Nah, we are good. You have been there more than a time or two for me. Plus, if I didn't handle it, you would have wreaked some havoc on that poor fella, and it would not have been pretty. I appreciate you letting us handle it," Tony said before he hung up the phone.

Steel smiled at the phone as he put it away and walked back into the locker room.

How does it feel? You have your first of many wins under your belt. What's next?"

Steel was elated. It was not until he looked at himself in the mirror that he noticed his eye was swelling. He also had a few bruises on his torso. Steel was riding high on this feeling. He never wanted it to end.

"To help ease your nerves, that other matter is taken care of. Nothing has surfaced, and it never will unless you decide that it needs to. Everyone is safe. I mean everyone," Stone assured Steel.

"Thank you," Steel put his fist up to Stone's already raised one. They bumped them and smiled.

"That reminds me someone wants to talk to you," Stone said, looking towards the door where Bronx stood waiting outside. At that moment, Bronx looks in through the small rectangular glass on the door, and Stone waves him in. "Alright, everybody out. Let's let the man catch his breath. He just had a great first fight." Turning to usher the others out, he called back over his shoulder that he would be at the gym if he needed him for anything.

Bronx walked a little unsteadily over to where Steel was. "Congratulations, kid. I thought you were going to lose it for a moment there when we first got here. But you did it." Bronx grimaced with every other step.

"Thanks, man. I am actually glad that you are here. We need to talk sooner rather than later." He paused briefly, drawing in a deep breath. "Today, things seem a little clearer than the last few days. If they are confusing for me, I can only imagine the same for you. Whatever this is, I need you to know that it is new to me. I feel something, but I do not know what it is. I have always been told that this is wrong. I said that to say, I can't promise you anything, but I would like the chance to get to know you without all the pressure of labels, if that makes sense to you."

Bronx had been quiet, taking in everything Steel was saying. "I never meant to cause things to get awkward, and I never meant to get you caught up in that mess with Spyder." He hesitated before continuing.

"I feel as if I should explain, especially if we are going to proceed. It started off as a means to keep my family safe. Then I started getting to know you. Once that happened, I tried to stall them as much as I could. I wanted to tell you what was going on a few times, but I could not, and I am so sorry. I was not strong enough to stand up to them, and they knew it."

Bronx started smiling. "If only you knew how many beatings, I took because of you. But I do not regret it. Only that I did not come to you or Stone sooner. By the way, that guy is a beast. When he calls in favors, he calls in favors. Spyder had no idea what was coming for him. I wish I could have been there for the look on Spyder's face when the police found him. He and his business have taken a hit. All I can say is that man has a lot of pull and respect."

"He has been pretty great to me, and for the life of me, I don't know why. Speaking of the beatings you took because of me, are you sure you are, okay?" Bronx nodded.

Steel stands up slowly and opens his arms so that he can embrace Bronx.

Without hesitation, Bronx steps in closer and smiles. As he pulled away. "This is not something I have done a lot of either, but I do know who I am."

Steel smiled. "We will see what happens. One day at a time." This was the first time in a while that Steel felt optimistic about his future. He had a family of brothers, a few sisters, and the possibility of someone who genuinely cared for him. The future excited him.

The End

Although DaKiara is still considered new to the publishing world, she has hit the ground running full speed ahead. In her first year, she independently published her first work. Soon after, she decided to form Mind Flow Publishing LLC, a small publishing house, to work with other authors. DaKiara has recently earned a spot on the Amazon International Bestsellers List. She has become a frequent flyer on the Amazon US Bestsellers List. Each time for her feels as if it is the first all over again. Her works are spread across genres such as Poetry, Inspirational, Urban Fiction, Paranormal, Contemporary Romance, Suspense & Thriller, and Christian Fiction.

In addition to having books available in paperback, and eBook formats, DaKiara has an ever-growing catalog on Amazon's newest platform, Vella. Some of those titles are Inn Too Deep, Split Decision, and Finding Kate. These have been some of her more popular projects. All are completed and will be moving to eBook and paperback in 2023.

DaKiara's love for writing started when she was

about twelve, writing poetry and writing speeches for various oratorical contests. Inspiration for her craft is pulled from her own life experiences, as well as others. She has been featured on several podcasts, as well as Up and Coming Authors Newsletters. When she is not writing, she loves to design shadowboxes and create personalized greeting cards.

Thank You for Reading....

facebook.com/carlette.thompsonwhitlock

twitter.com/DakiaraP

instagram.com/iamthelyte

tiktok.com/@iamdakiara

amazon.com/stores/author/B07D6GMLPK

linkedin.com/in/carlette-whitlock-889937179

bookbub.com/authors/dakiara

Also By DaKiara

The Mary B Chronicles

For Her Love

Standalone Short Stories

Charisma's Homecoming

Dreams Do Come True

A Chance at Love

Young Adult

Royalty

Occult & Horror

To Be Chosen

Inspirational

Journey to Living

Poetry

UPCOMING PROJECTS BY DAKIARA

- Secrets Uncovered Series
- Sleepless Nights (1)
- Dark Truths (2)
- Redeeming Justice (3)
- Sins of the Past (4)
- Balance of Power (5)
- For Her Love 2
- Dragon Slayer
- The Birthday Wish
- Inn Too Deep
- Sophie's Pack
- Split Decision
- Finding Kate

All titles will be available on Vella. All titles will be in eBook and paperback formats once completed.